AF491410

This Is Not Love at First Sight

A COZY FANTASY ROMANCE

BROTHERS OF FAIRWITCH ISLE

TEE HARLOWE

One

ELOWYN

I wouldn't call myself rebellious. Perhaps adventurous was more the right word to describe me. To be fair, one had to be a little adventurous living in Fairwitch Isle, a town hidden from the rest of the world. That meant no one could enter—or leave, not without risks anyway.

I couldn't count how many times over the years I'd craved leaving this sleepy little town and forging my own path in the world, but I couldn't. Not when my family needed me. Not when our little tavern needed me. Not when it meant if I left, I might not be able to come back. Fairwitch didn't always let people back in if they decided to leave, and that wasn't a gamble I could take.

I stood behind the counter of our mostly empty tavern, sneaking a glance at the hooded man in the back. I didn't know him, which was unusual for Fairwitch Isle, where everyone knew everyone. His plate of mashed potatoes and boar links sat in front of me on the wooden bar top. I reached into my pocket, sending a cursory glance behind me toward the kitchen door before I grabbed my signature mix I'd been working on: a combination of dried rosemary, garlic, onion, and thyme. I sprinkled the mixture onto the potatoes, then mashed them before clearing my throat.

"That was bold," Wolfe said from the far end of the bar, where he was nursing a steaming cup of tea.

He used to come in here everyday and spend all day drinking. But he'd gotten his act together in the last few years, and now, even though he didn't drink anymore, he came in quite often. I suspected it was loneliness, not that Wolfe would ever admit to such a thing.

I set the little vial of seasoning on the counter and raised my chin. "I don't know what you're referring to."

He lifted a thick, dark brow and shoved a hand through his mop of brown hair. "I'm talking about whatever you just added to those potatoes. The mashed potato recipe that has been in your family for generations."

I winced at the reminder of how little my family liked change compared to how much I craved it.

"Will you shut up?" I hissed, glancing behind me at the door that led to the kitchen. A little circle window gave view of Nan, humming as she stirred a big cauldron of porridge, preparing for the morning crowd. Papa and Mama stood on either side of her, both of them with brows furrowed as they stared at the bare shelves, which we were having more and more trouble stocking as our sales declined.

I jabbed a finger at Wolfe. "You didn't see anything." I blew a strand of wavy brown hair from my forehead. It always seemed to escape the ponytail I wore.

Wolfe held up his hands. "I don't feel like getting stabbed by one of your nan's sharp knives, so you're right. I didn't see anything." He went back to drinking his tea, and I rolled my eyes, knowing my secret would be safe.

Wolfe was the notorious town grump who liked his solitude. I suspected out of everyone, he probably talked to me the most—other than maybe his brothers.

I grabbed the plate and walked around the counter and toward the man sitting at the round table in the back.

High wooden beams stretched overhead, crisscrossing, bright lanterns hanging from them with flickering light that shed our little tavern with warmth. I passed the hearth that stood in the middle, the stone chimney stretching to the ceiling, a bubbling cauldron of stew currently cooking for the evening crowd.

Nan was stubborn, and even though we'd all tried to tell her there was no need to make so much for patrons that wouldn't come, she refused to listen. We were wasting far too much food because she was stuck in the past, in a time when this tavern was thriving, full of chatter and customers.

"Good luck," Wolfe muttered. "Hope he likes whatever concoction you added."

I shot the burly guard a glare and continued on my way. I loved making new creations, exciting and different—my family? Not so much.

I couldn't see the man's face as I set his plate in front of him. "Here we are," I chirped, hoping he liked it. It was the first time I was trying this seasoning on potatoes.

I'd snuck them onto chicken and our braised lamb, and both had been hits with the customers, not that they'd known that I'd done anything differently. But both tables had raved about the food, swearing they'd be back soon. Of course, I couldn't be consistent about it, so they had come back and ordered the same thing. But Nan had been hovering when I'd prepared the plates, and I'd run out of the seasoning, so I'd delivered the same old family recipe, much to the customers' disappointment. They hadn't been back since.

It was a risk, adding new spices and ingredients to Nan's creations, but I couldn't help it. Every other business in Fairwitch adapted, changed, grew—except us. We stayed stubbornly in the past, and it was killing our business. When people couldn't leave a town, they craved something new. We could give that to them. We could do weekly menus based on what our farmers had. We could put daily specials up. We could be the different they craved, the different that I craved. But it was useless. Nan thought it was a betrayal to our ancestors to change their ancient recipes.

The man nodded and murmured a thank you. I didn't move, arching my neck a little, waiting with anticipation to see him try the spiced potatoes. I'd also added a pat of butter behind Nan's back and a few grates of parmesan—a new cheese the local dairy shop had been experimenting with. Nan had wrinkled her nose when I'd burst into the tavern, parmesan wedge in hand. She'd told me it had no place in our business, but I was not about to let it go to waste.

The man cleared his throat, boot tapping on the floor. "Do you need something?"

His voice sounded oddly familiar, but I couldn't place it, especially when I couldn't see his face.

"No," I said with an awkward chuckle, backing away. "I'll just"—I hooked my thumb over my shoulder—"be right over there if you need me."

I spun on my heel and walked back toward the counter.

"That wasn't awkward," Wolfe said.

"Don't you have a brother to guard?" I asked with an edge to my voice.

Wolfe's brother just so happened to be the high prince of Fairwitch, and Wolfe was his personal guard, making it his mission to keep his brother safe. It was actually a bit of an obsession that I suspected stemmed from his younger brother's death years ago. Wolfe blamed himself and now would do anything to protect his other brother.

Wolfe just grunted into his almost empty mug. "Hard to protect my brother when he keeps sneaking off like a child instead of a thirty-year-old man who's in charge of an entire city." I laughed, and Wolfe sent me a withering glare. "It's not funny. I can't keep him safe from attacks if I don't know where he is. He doesn't take his safety seriously. Doesn't take anything seriously."

And I suspected Prince Cillian would say that his brother took everything far too seriously.

I frowned, looking up toward the vaulted wood ceiling. The attacks on Fairwitch had been increasing of late, and it had everyone on edge.

"Wind!" someone yelled, and my head snapped toward the large front windows, where gusts of wind were blowing villagers over.

The man in the back stiffened, and Wolfe shot to his feet, cursing under his breath. Another attack—this one apparently some kind of disastrous wind. My heart hammered as I watched everyone outside in a panic, fighting against the brutish winds.

"Stay here," Wolfe instructed as the wind rattled our windows, the gentle snowflakes that had been falling now swirling in fury. "Wait until the bells ring to go outside."

I nodded, watching Wolfe stalk out the door as a wintry blast barreled inside, knocking several chairs over before the door slammed shut.

Screams rang from outside as the royal guard ran through the streets. I hoped the high prince was safe. If I knew Wolfe, he was currently panicking over his brother's whereabouts.

"What's all that?" Nan appeared beside me, nodding her head toward the window.

"Another attack," I said.

"Another one?" Mama and Papa stood in the doorway of the kitchen.

Papa put his arm around my mother, drawing her close. "I'm sure the royal guard will get it under control."

"Have they figured out where the attacks are coming from yet?" Mama asked. "They've been happening for months now, and we still haven't caught who's doing this, who's using this magic against us."

Papa's lips turned downward.

"Well, if we do find out who's causing all the ruckus, I'm ready to fight." Nan lifted her gleaming butcher knife and smiled in a way that absolutely terrified me. "I'm not afraid to use this." She shook it in the air, and Mama rushed forward.

"Okay, Mother." She grabbed the knife. "Let's just put this down and save the fighting for the royal guard."

Nan harrumphed, snatching her knife back from my mother and knocking over the little glass vial of my special seasoning, spilling it all across the counter.

I stiffened as Nan's dark eyes sharpened, narrowing. She swiped a finger along the seasoning and brought it to her mouth.

Oh no. My seasoning. I'd meant to put it back into my pocket, but Wolfe had distracted me.

"Rosemary, thyme, onion." Gran smacked her lips together, her tone disapproving.

"And garlic," I added, wincing as Mama gasped.

"Have you been tinkering again?" She twirled a strand of brown hair, the same mahogany shade as mine, around a finger, though grey streaked hers.

"Please don't tell me you changed one of the recipes again," Papa said, looking up at the ceiling like he was praying to one of the godwitches for a different daughter, one who didn't insist on ruining generations of food.

"It's just a little pinch of seasoning." My gaze darted to the man eating, and pleasure flushed my cheeks as I noticed the potatoes were gone. "And some butter. And parmesan."

Nan thwacked her hand on the table. "Parmesan?"

Papa muttered under his breath and turned toward the statue of the food godwitch sitting on one of our shelves. "We're sorry she desecrated your food," he said.

My eyes rolled so far up I was sure they might get stuck in my head. The food and wine godwitch was the patron of our establishment, and we made regular offerings to them, hoping they would, in turn, keep our restaurant from closing. It was said that our line ran directly back to the food godwitch, that some of these recipes we served were their own original recipes from thousands of years ago.

"Elowyn, how could you?" Mama asked, eyes darting to the food godwitch like the statue might come alive and berate us for changing its potato recipe.

I set my hands on my hips. "It's not like I murdered someone and fed them to a customer."

Mama's mouth dropped open, alarm flickering in her brown eyes.

I stared at her for a moment. "I didn't actually kill someone, Mama. It's just seasoning."

"Just seasoning?" Nan snapped. "It's betrayal is what it is."

Mama nodded along, Papa squeezing his arm tight around her, the mustache on his upper lip twitching in annoyance.

This was ridiculous. This was why I had to do things like sneak seasonings into dishes. I should have stood up to them. I should have told them that the reason I snuck in seasonings and changed recipes behind their backs was because our restaurant would close soon if we didn't do something new. People were sick of the same old thing. But saying that would mean arguing, and I didn't want to argue or cause strife, so I adopted the most apologetic expression I could muster and said, "It won't happen again."

That was a lie. It would happen again. I couldn't help myself. If I didn't do something to change this ordinary, boring, repetitive existence of mine, I'd wither up and become a shell.

Nan nodded, her sharp chin jutting out in displeasure as Mama and Papa ushered her back into the kitchen. The bells rang out, signaling the latest threat had been vanquished, and I noticed the hooded man had slipped out at some point, a stack of gold coins sitting on the table, far more than what that dish had cost. He must've really liked the potatoes, then.

Snow blanketed the streets, and in the distance I could see the castle, the center of Fairwitch Isle.

Its white stone and glittering stained-glass windows stood stark against the snow around it. The view of the castle was just another gut punch, a reminder of all the ways I had failed. I could just imagine all the recipes I'd be whipping up if I'd gotten the royal chef position. With the salary, I could keep our tavern afloat and let Nan, Mama, and Papa keep on with their stubborn ways while I got to do something new and exciting.

But I didn't get the chef position. No, that had gone to Liam Wolvern. Just thinking his name sent fiery ropes of anger twisting through me. My lifelong nemesis, a man I despised for many reasons. And he was there right now in the castle, living my dream life as royal chef.

I peeked over my shoulder to make sure no one was looking, then popped open my little glass vial, scooped the spilled seasoning into it, and got back to work.

Two

LIAM

Snow fell in fat flurries outside the stained-glass windows of the castle kitchen, the edges of the panes little squares of blue and silver, while the insides remained clear, giving a full view of the castle gardens.

My knife fell in a rhythmic thunk, chopping through the carrot on the cutting board in front of me.

Chop. Chop. Chop.

I looked at the recipe lying on the counter, making sure I was following each step in the exact order listed.

"Where are we at with the chicken pot pie?" A voice floated down through the dumbwaiter in the brick wall next to me.

I ran a hand through my hair, and despite the cold wind rattling the window panes, sweat gathered on my forehead.

I swiped it with the back of my arm. Fuck. I stared at the paper in front of me, losing my place and forgetting what step I was at.

"It's coming," I called to Louisa.

"Well, the prince is getting hungry," she said.

I glanced out the window again, the sun setting, the sky a brilliant purple and pink. It was past his dinnertime, and I'd gotten so caught up reading and checking over these steps a million times, I hadn't kept to schedule. This was a new recipe, and I'd wanted to make sure I'd gotten it right.

New recipes always caused me anxiety. I liked the tried and true ones, the recipes I knew by heart, that I didn't have to learn. But the prince had tried some pot pie dish at a restaurant in town and loved it so much he wanted me to make it for him.

I grabbed the parchment the recipe was scribbled on with a trembling hand.

"Uh oh," a voice said from outside the door. "Someone's late with dinner."

I rolled my eyes at the hulking stone gargoyle statues that sat on either side of the kitchen door, snow piling on the horns atop their heads. Tal and Barty were some of the castle's more annoying magical quirks, twin gargoyle statues who came to life and loved to hear themselves talk.

I scooped up the chopped carrots and threw them into a sizzling pan, a pool of lard already melted.

I checked the fire under the stove, which was roaring thanks to the castle's magic. It always kept the stove exactly the right temperature, which made my job a lot easier.

"Prince Cillian gets grumpy when dinner's late," Barty, the gargoyle on the left, said.

A knife floated over my head, thunking down to start slicing the raw lumps of chicken sitting on a different cutting board. The castle's magic made it feel like I had my very own sous chef, one that anticipated all my needs.

"I don't have time for either of you." I grabbed a clove of garlic, mincing it. "Don't you have doors to be opening?"

That was the gargoyles' main purpose. They opened doors—the front doors, the doors to the high prince's chambers, the door to my kitchen, the door to the greenhouse. But, sometimes, when they were bored, they liked to appear outside my kitchen door and bother me.

"Nope," Barty said. "Snow's falling. Everyone's in for the night."

"Including the prince," Tal said from the other side of the door. "And I heard his stomach grumbling from all the way down here."

"That was my line," Barty said. "We rehearsed it, and I was the one who was going to say that."

"Well, I changed my mind and thought it sounded better coming from me," Tal said.

Godwitches be. I could not handle their bickering right now. I needed silence so I could concentrate on getting this meal, which was very late, to the prince.

"Can I get a snack for the prince?" Louisa said into the dumbwaiter.

I groaned and grabbed a handful of roasted chestnuts, throwing them into a bowl and putting them on the little wooden tray. "It's ready!"

The tray lifted on its own, the castle's magic at work as it pulled the tray upward to where Louisa would be waiting.

"Don't poke me!" Barty was yelling at Tal.

"I'll poke you if I want to," Tal said back.

"Enough!" I slammed my hands hard enough that both gargoyles jumped, and the knife slicing the chicken clattered to the table. "I have dinner to make. I don't have time for your petty arguments."

"Someone is testy," Tal said.

"See if we ever open your door for you again," Barty added.

The gargoyles spread their wings and flew off to some other part of the castle where they would no longer be bothering me.

The pan behind me popped and sizzled, a burning smell infiltrating my nostrils.

Oh, fuck.

I whirled to see the onion, carrots, and celery blackening on the stovetop. This was why I couldn't deal with distractions. If I was distracted, things inevitably went wrong.

I ran to the stove and shoved an oven mitt on before grabbing the pan and setting it on a rag laid out on the counter, but it was too late. The veggies were burned to a crisp, and I'd have to start all over.

The door to the kitchen opened, an icy chill bursting in, the flames in the hearth flickering with the howling wind.

I shivered as snowflakes swirled in a flurry around the kitchen.

"There's my boy," Father said as he shut the door behind him. He took off his cloak and shook out the snowflakes.

A mop sashayed over, cleaning up the melted snow before anyone could slip on it. The mop could clean and the knife could chop, but the pan couldn't lift off the stove when the veggies were done? I shot a glare at it behind me, hating the unpredictability of the castle's magic. It decided when and where and how it wanted to use it, and there was absolutely no rhyme or reason to any of it. So, sure sometimes it felt like I had a reliable sous chef. Other times, it felt like I had a drunk sous chef helping me.

"What are you doing here?" I asked my father, moving to stand in front of the burnt remains of the high prince's dinner. The last thing I needed was my father seeing that and reprimanding me, reminding me how I was the last of his legacy, the last chance for a Wolvern to get the job of royal chef.

It didn't matter that I had won the job. No, I had to continually prove my worth, prove that I was the best chef on the continent and especially better than Elowyn Carragh.

He stroked his short, grey beard, jaw locking, and I instantly knew something was bothering him. Nothing new there. Most of what I did bothered my father, and I'd learned to not care what he thought of me anymore. I did his bidding, being the royal chef—not because I was afraid of what he thought but because I was all he had left, and it would break his heart if I didn't follow through on this dream of his for his son to be the royal chef. For all my father's flaws, he'd always been there for me and my sister. Had always loved us, provided a safe, happy life for us. I owed this to him, even if it meant my stomach was usually twisted into a tight knot.

Maybe I could get a run in later.

He swiped some snowflakes from his shoulder-length grey hair. "I heard a rumor that the prince is looking for a new chef."

I froze, shoulders bunching at the tremble in his voice. I would definitely need that run, snow or not. "I'm sure it's just a rumor. You know how gossip spreads in Fairwitch, and half of it isn't even close to true."

This was so fucking important to my father, and I'd only had the job for a year, already feeling like I was messing it up every step of the way. I shot a look behind me, wincing at the sight of the blackened veggies. I loved cooking—that had never been the problem. The problem was all this pressure. The business of this kitchen. When I was cooking at our family bakery, it was simple, easier.

I could add new ingredients to cakes, cookies, tarts, pies, try new flavors, but the basic recipes never changed. I could handle that. Here in the castle kitchen, I had to plan huge feasts, cook for the high prince and his family, make meals and snacks on a whim—all with a sentient castle and its spontaneous magic at work. There was no routine, no order, and I absolutely hated it. But I couldn't admit that to my father.

My father sniffed the air, nose wrinkling. "Is something burning?"

"Uh." I scratched my head as Louisa's voice floated down the dumbwaiter right next to where my father was standing.

"The high prince has decided to dine out today. He'll have the pot pie tomorrow."

My father looked between the dumbwaiter and me, then stalked toward me and shoved me aside, groaning as he set his gaze upon the burnt remains of the prince's dinner.

"I got distracted," I admitted. "The fucking gargoyles. They love to lurk outside and chatter, and it makes it hard to concentrate."

Father pinched the bridge of his nose. "Every royal chef in the history of this castle has had to deal with the gargoyles."

Here we went. Anytime I brought up a concern, my father was quick to remind me that everyone else in the history of Fairwitch dealt with it just fine, so I should too. And he wasn't wrong. I should've been able to handle these things. I should've been able to handle distractions and surprises and spontaneity.

Elowyn Carragh would have.

But I didn't want to think about her, didn't want to think about how much better suited for this role she was than me. And I definitely didn't want to think about how my father might very well die of a broken heart if the high prince really was looking for a new chef—and she got the job.

I felt so deficient sometimes. Like something was wrong with me because my brain didn't seem to work like everyone else's.

My father was still talking, in the middle of a story, when I started listening again. "Your grandmother had to cook an entire feast while dealing with the stove catching on fire because the castle got grumpy about her making—"

"A dish with sardines," I finished for him.

I'd heard this story a hundred times. No one had ever dared use sardines since. Apparently the castle hated the smell, and when you lived in a sentient castle that could make you disappear deep in its depths, you paid attention to what it liked and didn't like.

"Exactly." My father spread out his arms. "If your grandmother could handle a fire in the kitchen and make a feast still talked about decades later, then you can cook with some talking gargoyles. Just shut them out, son."

"Is there a reason you're here?" I asked as the door burst open again, a wintery mix barreling in.

"The prince is looking for a new chef!" Ava stood in the doorway, chest heaving. My little sister looked far too delighted with this news.

"So I've heard," I said.

She shut the door behind her, shaking out her long blonde hair that was the same golden shade as mine.

"Don't you have schoolwork to be doing?" I asked with a raised brow, but Ava ignored me, coming to stand by our father.

"Apparently, he's eating at The Deerborn right now."

I stiffened, knowing that was the worst thing she could've said and also knowing she'd probably done it on purpose. Unlike me, Ava loved to irk our father.

The Deerborn was Elowyn's family restaurant, and if the prince was eating there . . . No. No, he wouldn't just offer a job to Elowyn without even talking to me first.

My father clutched his chest, taking a few steps backward, wrinkled face paling. "Oh, this is bad. None of the Wolvern chefs have ever gotten fired. Except for—"

"Perla Wolvern," both Ava and I said at the same time.

The black sheep of the family. She got fired when it was discovered she was poisoning the high prince and queen in small doses, trying to kill them because that was how badly she wanted to be free of the job, and apparently, trying to murder them was easier than just telling her family. That was how insane the Wolverns were.

"What do I do?" I asked, out of options. I couldn't lose this job and ruin our family legacy, not when I felt like my entire purpose in life was to fulfill it.

"We're going to figure out if this rumor is true," he said. "Time for a visit to the Deerborn."

Three

A blanket of white covered the streets of Fairwitch, and I trudged my way through the ankle-deep snow, carrying a bag of veggies and fruits I'd gotten from our local greenhouse. The same fruits and veggies I got every week.

My cloak blew behind me in the frigid wind, and I shivered, feeling the cold in every crevice of my body, my face and ears aching from the bite of it.

Children played in the streets, snowballs flying through the air, and I passed a snowman with a carrot for a nose and black buttons as eyes and a mouth.

I recognized the girl building it: Ava Wolvern, Liam's little sister.

Her golden hair hung in a braid down her back, and she and some of her friends put the finishing touches on the snowman. Ava grabbed the hat off her friend's head and plopped it on top of their creation.

"There," she said, "he's finished."

I wasn't sure exactly how old she was, but if I had to guess, I'd place her at around fifteen. Young and with her whole future ahead of her. It was pathetic that I was jealous of a fifteen-year-old girl. I was twice her age, and instead of living my best life, all I felt was stuck. Figuratively and literally. I looked down at my boot, currently wedged in a deep spot of snow. I groaned and attempted to yank my foot out.

"So have you decided when you're going to do it?" one of Ava's friends asked. Mary was her name if I remembered correctly.

"Shhh," Ava said, and I couldn't help but lean a little closer.

If I couldn't live my life the way I wanted, maybe I could live vicariously through these teenagers.

Pathetic. So, so pathetic.

"Shhh," Ava said. "I told you that's a secret."

"I just want to know when you're going to do it," Mary whispered.

Do what? I leaned closer. This was getting juicy.

"Okay, fine. After the Winter Solstice."

"And your father and brother don't know?"

"That's the whole point. If they knew, they'd never allow it. But I need to get out of this place or I'm going to be stuck here forever."

Her words hit me right in the heart. Was Ava planning on running away? One the one hand, I was jealous, longing for that kind of adventure and courage. On the other hand . . . should I tell someone? Ava was fifteen, and she was too young to go out on her own. If she were five years older, I wouldn't bat an eye, but this sounded like a bad idea.

The thing was I couldn't exactly tell her family. My gaze flew to the bakery, right next to the Deerborn, the two buildings conjoined so it looked like they might be a joint business. Once upon a time, they were—before the wooden wall that got put up between us, separating the two spaces. If I tried to tell Liam or his father about this, I doubted they'd listen. It would also cause more friction between our families, something we didn't need, not when tensions were at an all-time high.

I finally yanked my foot out of the snow right when Nan burst out of the Deerborn, waving a letter in the air. "Elowyn, Elowyn, you'll never believe what just came!"

I'd worry about Ava later. Maybe I could talk to her myself without anyone else knowing. She didn't seem to hold the same grudge as her father and brother, didn't glower at me whenever we crossed paths.

Nan ran out to me, not even wearing a cloak, the grey bun on her head bobbing.

"Nan! It's freezing out here."

I met her outside the Deerborn as she shoved the envelope in my face. "You got an invitation to the Winter Solstice feast."

I wrinkled my nose. "That's why you ran out here? Everyone gets that invitation, Nan. That's the whole point. It's a feast for all of Fairwitch to attend."

"No, no, no. You don't understand. The invitation isn't to attend. It's to cook for it. You're invited to cook in the castle kitchen."

I dropped the bags of food I was holding, barely hearing them thump in the snow. "W-what?" I heard myself say, my voice sounding muffled and squeaky. "I don't understand."

Nan raised her voice, and I shot a look over the short stone wall that separated our patio from the Sweet Treat—the Wolverns's bakery. "Apparently, it's such a monumental task, they want to bring in help."

Understanding hit me. That was why Nan was out here. She wanted the Wolverns to hear this. And it worked.

Eamon Wolvern appeared, shoulder-length grey hair blowing in the wind as he scowled at my nan. "Quiet, woman," he barked. "You're disturbing my customers. You'd know patrons don't like yelling if you ever had any of your own."

Nan stepped toward the wall. Oh no. Last time she and Eamon had gotten into a screaming match, the royal guard had to come and throw them in the dungeons for an entire day due to disorderly conduct.

I hadn't witnessed it, but Mama claimed Nan had threatened to castrate Eamon with one of her knives.

"Times are tough," Nan argued.

Eamon gestured to his bakery, brimming full of customers sitting and eating their baked goods and drinking tea. "Not for us." He arched his neck. "Just for you, apparently."

I grabbed Nan's arm, afraid my invitation would be rescinded if she and Eamon got into yet another screaming match. She wrenched her arm away, ignoring me completely.

I tried to peek into the dark windows of our tavern, wondering where Mama and Papa were. Probably somewhere in the back, preparing the midday meal. Could sure use their help right about now.

I squeaked when I turned and realized Nan and Eamon were now nose-to-nose, with only that short stone wall separating them, and Nan would have no problem jumping it. She was surprisingly agile for her ripe age of eighty.

"How dare you," Eamon was saying. "My ancestors would never stoop to steal one of your recipes. As if we'd need to."

"Oh, please." Nan jabbed a finger into his chest. "We all know that's why Mikhail Wolvern was the first royal chef in the Fairwitch Castle. He stole my great-great-great-great Aunt Liadon's recipe."

"No he didn't." Spittle flew from Eamon's mouth. "She stole his!"

They'd had this same argument at least a hundred times. It was the family lore—what had started the rivalry between the Wolverns and the Carraghs in the first place. The story went that Fairwitch was established by our elders, and the city was ruled by the Fairwitch, leader of all the godwitches. She built this magnificent castle and wanted a royal chef, deciding to hold a competition for the role. The story had gotten so twisted over time, both sides accusing the other of cheating, poisoning, stealing.

"It was your murderous ancestor who poisoned Mikhail, then took his recipe," Eamon shouted.

"Father!" Ava ran to her father's side, shooting me what I thought was an eye roll. "Come inside."

Her father listened to her about as well as Nan did to me, shaking his daughter off.

"Liadon didn't poison Mikhail." Nan spit in the snow. "She didn't have to. Mikhail was failing at his job, and then had the unfortunate misfortune to get ill. Liadon simply took over and did a better job."

Eamon gasped. "You shouldn't speak ill of the dead."

"I don't think that's what she was doing—" Ava tried, but Nan interrupted.

"I'll speak ill of the dead if they deserve it. And Mikhail Wolvern absolutely deserves it. He stole her recipe and that's the only reason he won that competition." She raised her nose in the air. "Liadon wasn't second best at all."

Eamon's face had turned so red I thought he might pass out.

"And Elowyn won't be second best to your son now that she's been invited to cook at the castle."

Eamon froze, and Ava's mouth dropped open, gaze flicking to me.

I cleared my throat and gave a small wave. "Surprise."

"The castle won't let her enter the kitchen," Eamon said.

Fear threaded my veins. What if he was right? The sentient castle was known to be picky, sometimes not letting certain residents of Fairwitch enter, and no one knew why it made the choices it did. If it didn't let me enter, this new opportunity would be gone before I even had a chance to seize it. I hadn't realized until Eamon said it how desperately I wanted this.

It could finally be my chance to get out of the tavern and leave this dreary, boring life behind before it was too late, before it completely suffocated me.

"Oh, I think it will." Nan shook the letter in the air. "This is a letter from the high prince himself inviting her. Apparently he was our mystery diner last night." She gave me a look, and I gasped. He was the one who'd eaten my potatoes?

Eamon tried to snatch the parchment from her, but she clutched it to her chest. "I wonder if the high prince is displeased with the current cook."

I thought of Liam, his smug, arrogant attitude, how he'd always acted like he was better than me, and I couldn't help feel a little mollified by this invitation, by Nan's words. No one in the history of the royal chefs had needed another chef to help prepare the Winter Solstice meal. This was a first, and if the high prince was inviting me, there must've been a reason. I just couldn't imagine Liam fumbling this opportunity. He'd been the royal chef for almost a year now, getting the role after my aunt retired from the job.

We'd all hoped I would be her successor, but perfect Liam Wolvern had ended up getting the job over me, and it had torn me to shreds, filled me with so much self doubt, and it was just recently I'd started experimenting again, finding the courage to put my own stamp on this world.

But now this opportunity might be a chance for me to prove myself, for me to take the role that I so desperately wanted.

"She isn't going to need to!" Gran was yelling, jabbing her finger in Eamon's face and ripping me back to the present. "She'll be on her side of the kitchen, and he'll be on his."

"I'm drawing a line on the kitchen floor!" Eamon shouted. "Right down the middle. She can't cross to his side." He sniffed. "Liam wouldn't want to cross to hers."

"Father," Ava tried, but he held up a hand and cut her off.

"Fine with me!" Nan shouted.

This was getting ridiculous. I wondered if this was how I'd act at their age. Liam and I might have not liked each other, but we'd never gotten into screaming matches like this. And while I didn't like Liam, I knew we couldn't each take a half of the kitchen and stay there. There was no world in which that would work.

Nan held up a finger. "And they'll communicate through the servants and assistants. No need to speak a word to each other."

"Liam wouldn't dare speak to her anyway," Eamon muttered.

"Huh, well that's too bad since he could learn a lot from my Elowyn." Nan patted my shoulder as my cheeks heated, even out in the blustery cold.

"Then it's settled." Eamon raised his chin. "You stay away from my son and from his position." This time the words were directed at me, but it wasn't anger I detected in Eamon's voice. It was fear, which made no sense. What did he have to fear? His bakery was thriving. If his son lost the royal chef position, they'd still have a booming family business.

Whereas if I didn't prove myself in that kitchen, we might lose ours.

One thing was clear: things were about to get very, very messy.

Four

ELOWYN

I walked through the castle gardens, frost covering the flowers and trees. My footprints made a path as I followed the trail toward the little rectangular building sticking out the side of the castle, a chimney smoking from its snow-blanketed roof. My breath puffed out in front of me, but nerves jangled in my stomach, and I barely even felt the cold.

My recipe journal was clutched in my hand, all my ideas over the years tucked into the pages. So many dreams and hopes and culinary adventures I'd never gotten to explore. The Winter Solstice would be the perfect time to bring out some of these ideas, maybe even impress Nan, Mama, and Papa enough that they'd be willing to change some of the recipes at Deerborn.

If Liam Wolvern would allow it, that was. Despite the high prince's invitation, this was still his kitchen, and the letter had made it clear I'd be reporting to Liam, that he'd have the final say on all the dishes we were planning.

I gazed at the sprawling white-stone castle that towered over the kitchen. Stained-glass windows added pops of bright color, and winter-hardy potted violas dotted all the balconies.

I'd attended the winter feast every year since I was born. It was the only time I ever stepped foot inside the castle, and I'd only seen the dining hall.

My gaze moved back to the little building sticking out the side. Never the kitchen.

I'd heard about the castle kitchen from Nan, of course. Her father had been royal chef around eighty years ago, and she loved regaling me with stories about coming to the castle kitchen and seeing her father cook. How she'd watch him chop so fast she was worried he'd cut off a thumb—but he never did. Thankfully.

While Gran's childhood had been spent in the castle, mine had been spent sitting in the Deerborn, watching Gran chop and sauté and mix, wishing desperately I could see the castle kitchen for myself. And now I'd finally get the chance.

I wished it didn't have to be with Liam Wolvern, but I wouldn't let him ruin this experience. He could glower all he wanted, scoff at my ideas, ridicule me, but nothing could dampen this experience, and by the end of it, maybe I'd have a permanent position here.

A blast of wintery wind barreled around me, the air crisp, the town silent as everyone was no doubt in their homes, cozying up in front of their fires and out of the cold. I hated Fairwitch like this. I missed the hustle and bustle, the chatter, the laughter.

I approached the kitchen, its walls made of white gleaming stone like the rest of the castle with shimmering blue stained-glass windows, a little spatula and chef knife carved on two of the panels. I couldn't count how many times I'd come into the castle gardens to stare at the kitchen, to imagine myself in there one day.

Excitement bubbled in my stomach, replacing my nerves as I approached the little wooden door, reaching out to open it.

"What do you think you're doing?"

I shrieked and jumped back, staring at the gargoyle statue that had just spoken. There were two of them, one of either side of the door.

He—it?—tilted his head, two curved horned atop it, sharp enough to impale someone.

I'd forgotten about the gargoyles since I hardly ever came to the castle, but they were the official . . . door openers? I wasn't really sure what title they held. All I knew was that they opened doors for people.

I grabbed the end of my ponytail. "Sorry. I guess that's your job."

"Oh no." The gargoyle on the left crossed his arms. "Don't mind me. Go ahead and take the one thing I'm good at away from me."

The gargoyle on the right looked over at him. "You're not actually that good at it, Barty."

They had names. Somehow I'd never known that the statue gargoyles had actual names. I also hadn't known they bickered like an old married couple.

Barty's head snapped to the side. "What are you talking about, Tal?"

The other gargoyle shrugged. "You just don't have that finesse about you."

"Finesse?" Barty echoed.

I was going to be late at this point, and perfect Liam Wolvern would absolutely hold that over my head. I raised a finger. "Excuse me, I'd really like to get into the kitchen now if you don't mind."

Both gargoyles turned to stare at me, apparently having forgotten my presence entirely.

"I'm the new chef," I said.

Barty gasped. "But Liam is the chef."

Tal stared at its long talons. "I never really liked him anyway. He's always too 'busy' to talk."

That sounded like Liam, alright. I was glad I wasn't the only one who saw behind the perfection to someone who, at their core, thought they were better than everyone else.

I stepped forward, reaching for the door handle when Barty's hand snaked out, wrapping around my wrist, stone hard and cold.

"I thought we already established that that's our job."

"Well, if you were better at your job, she wouldn't have had to do that." Tal looked pointedly straight ahead.

Not this again. I was never going to get into this damn kitchen, and it wouldn't even be because the kitchen wouldn't let me in—it would be because of the statues who couldn't stop arguing long enough to open a door.

"Why do you have to be so mean all the time?" Barty let go of my hand, and I slowly backed away as their bickering continued.

I couldn't get in through the door, which was the only entrance to the kitchen. There was no door from the castle into the kitchen. Gran had told me all food got sent up the dumbwaiter, which I couldn't wait to see.

I eyed the window, noticing the slightest gap between it and the frame. Maybe it was unlocked. That could actually work. I'd snuck out of plenty of windows during my rebellious teenage years.

I plastered myself to the stone wall like I was a spy on a mission and inched toward the window. I definitely was not a teenager anymore. Nowadays, if I slept wrong, I woke up with crick in my neck, but what choice did I have? The gargoyles wouldn't let me in. Liam most certainly wouldn't let me in. So I had to figure this out myself.

I faced the window, admiring the pretty stained glass that framed the pane, the sun so bright and glaring I couldn't see inside. I had no idea if anyone was even in there, even noticed me.

Hopefully they didn't notice me. It would be better for everyone if I could just slip in quietly, introduce myself, and then get to work.

Dark grey clouds covered the sun, snow beginning to fall. I needed to get inside now before I froze to death.

Not wasting any more time, I wedged my fingers in the window and pried it open, then heaved myself up. Or tried to, anyway. My upper body strength wasn't what it used to be.

I grunted, once again attempting to lift myself, but it wasn't working. So I opted for swinging my leg up. Oh, godwitches. That was definitely a position my leg was not meant to be in.

My body stretched tight, and I worried I'd snapped a ligament. I couldn't stop now, so I did an awkward sort of flip into the kitchen, the window rattling behind me.

Except I didn't land on my feet. I rolled right into open air and slammed into a body. We both tumbled to the floor, and I didn't even have to look to know who I'd just landed on top of. I'd sat next to him for almost fifteen years of school. I knew the freshly baked bread scent mixed with hints of smokey ash.

Liam stared up at me with his wide brown eyes. Those stupid eyes that were so dark and expressionless. I could never read them, never see the emotion in them, which only furthered my suspicion about him being a sociopath.

"What in the fuck, Elowyn?" he asked in that voice, the same judgmental tone he'd always used when it came to me.

He'd been doing it since our early years in school together.

That's not how you do that, Elowyn.

You forgot your parchment and quill again?

You have ink on your shirt.

Oh, look who finally showed up to class.

It felt like he was constantly judging me, judging everything I did, and it had only added to my dislike of him over the years.

"Your gargoyles wouldn't let me in," I said, realizing I was straddling him, my thighs clenched tight around his waist, my hands pressed to his chest, which—hello, muscles.

I scrambled to a stand, and he slowly got to his feet, straightening to his full height that towered over me, his chiseled jaw locked.

"You could've broken the window." He walked over and latched it.

I crossed my arms. "I could've broken my body!"

Snowflakes had swirled in, dropping to the ground, and a mop drifted over, sopping up the mess. They had their own magic mop? What I wouldn't give to not have to mop or sweep the tavern again.

"You do realize we have a door, right?" Liam's arm swept toward the closed wooden door that a set of short stairs led down to, both gargoyles still outside and still bickering.

"I told you the gargoyles wouldn't let me enter." I picked up my notebook that had fallen on the floor, slamming it onto the counter. "I realize there is a door. Unfortunately, I had to find alternative options."

Liam's face screwed up in confusion. "Why didn't you just knock and let me know you were here?"

I scoffed. Was this guy for real? "Yeah, sure. You'd have let me in. The same person who wouldn't even let me use his ink pot when I ran out in school. Just yesterday, my gran and your father were having a screaming match about drawing a line through the kitchen to ensure neither of us sullied the other's workspace. I'm sure your father told you all about it. So, no, I don't believe you'd open a door for me."

Liam shoved a hand through his golden hair, and it fell right back into perfect waves on his head, a few cowlicks falling over his eyes. "I told my father his idea wouldn't work." He nodded his head toward the floor. "Do you see any lines?"

No, no I didn't, but that didn't change the fact that Liam and I came from families who hated each other, who thrived on that hatred. It was what fueled us to become the royal chef, our two family lines dueling it out generation after generation. I didn't believe for a second he was going to let me through that kitchen door.

"Either way, we need to get to work." Liam shot a concerned glance out the window. "The snow is really falling, isn't it?"

I looked behind me. "It usually does in winter."

Liam sighed. "We're going to be working together a lot in the next week, so we need to put aside all the family bullshit and put our best foot forward. It's the only way we'll deliver an amazing winter feast."

"I agree," I said, even though I hated the way the words tasted on my tongue. I didn't want to work with Liam. I wanted to beat Liam, to show him up after years of dealing with his arrogance, his conviction that he was better than me.

I took a deep breath, remembering my goal. It wasn't to be friends with Liam. It wasn't to get him to like me or see me differently. It was to take his job, and to do that, we did need to work together. Or, at least, I needed to pretend while wowing the high prince.

"Let's restart," I suggested, taking a moment to ground myself. "I think we got off on the wrong foot."

I took a deep breath and soaked in my surroundings. I was in the royal kitchen. After a lifetime of dreaming about this moment, I was here. I glanced around the small brick room, stepping toward the hearth, warmth emanating from the crackling fire. I walked around the outer edge of the room, running my fingers over the wooden counter-tops with all the grooves and rivets.

I gasped and stopped at the four-burner cast iron stove, a little fire chamber underneath.

We had a one-burner stove at our tavern, but I could just imagine how much I could cook at once with four whole burners. A clay oven sat in the corner, a long spout rising from it and up into the ceiling. I could bake at least four loaves of bread at a time in that thing.

The outside walls might have been white stone, but inside brick made up the walls, all different shades of brown, red, and orange, giving a warmth to the kitchen that I could sink into.

"We have a lot to do," Liam said, voice curt. "So if you're done with the tour?"

So much for restarting.

The scent of thyme and rosemary floated through the air, and I noticed the mound of dough on the wooden island next to the chopped herbs.

"I thought we could start with the bread," Liam said. "We make all the dough ahead of time and put it in the ice box, then move on to chopping the veggies that we can also put in the ice box. We're going to be feeding hundreds of people. I have a whole list of all the servants who will be helping us and already assigned them with tasks . . ."

His voice faded into the background as I stared at the dough, getting that familiar tingle. The one that had me itching to try something new. Every year at Winter Solstice, we had the same thyme and rosemary bread. But what if we tried something different this year? We could do a braided bread, one strand with rosemary and the other with thyme, and then we could do a dipping sauce. Or maybe some softened, whipped butter with parmesan flakes. My mouth watered at the possibilities of it all.

"What are you doing?" Liam asked.

My head snapped up, and I realized I was already rolling the bread into separate strands. "I have some ideas," I admitted.

"Ideas?" Liam started pacing. "You can't just come in here with ideas." He shook the parchment paper that no doubt was full of his lists. "We have a plan. A plan we need to stick to if we want to pull off this winter feast."

My anger flared. This was exactly what he always did. Shot me down. "Well, apparently, your plans aren't working all that well. Otherwise, I wouldn't have been invited to help you cook."

Liam stepped back like I'd slapped him, his golden skin losing some of its color. "Maybe our families were right. We can't work together." He shoved a piece of parchment toward me and nodded toward a white apron hanging on a hook. "Put that on, then get to work. Here's the recipe. We're going to need about twenty loaves. Start mixing. I'll be over here, chopping." He nodded toward a counter as far away from me as possible.

Just like that, he'd sliced me open, all my excitement bleeding away like it did every day at the Deerborn.

I should've known this would happen. I took my idea notebook and stuffed it into my apron, looking at the recipe in front of me and following the instructions while doing my best to ignore Liam for the rest of the day.

Five

Liam

Snow continued to fall in a heavy curtain, blocking the view of the castle gardens, the kitchen dark without sun spilling in. Candles flickered along the walls, and the roaring fire in the hearth made the space feel mostly warm—except for the icy cold stares coming from Elowyn.

When I'd found out she'd been invited to cook at the castle, I panicked. I had no idea what Prince Cillian was playing at. Maybe he wanted to see how Elowyn did because he was planning on firing me, which would devastate my father and be the worst kind of betrayal to him after a lifetime of preparing for this very thing, preparing to be successful at this very thing.

Elowyn hummed to herself, adding a sprinkle of flour to the table before she started rolling out the dough she'd made.

She always did this. Breezed through things like nothing mattered. She'd show up late to class constantly, plopping down next to me and asking what she'd missed while I was trying to pay attention.

She'd even managed to get me in trouble a few times, the teacher accusing me of talking when I was trying to tell Elowyn to be quiet. She'd just laughed, mischief dancing in those moss-green eyes. She'd always loved watching me suffer. I supposed that was the whole point of our family rivalry.

Tears pricked my eyes as I began chopping an onion, the overpowering scent wafting straight up my nostrils.

"Are you crying, Wolvern?" Elowyn asked.

I sniffed. "I'm chopping onions."

"Oh, too bad," she said and went back to kneading. "For a second, I thought I'd made you cry."

She was so irritating. She shook out her ponytail, her rich brown hair shimmering under the firelight, glimmers of red peeking through the brown strands.

"Aren't there servants coming to help?" she asked, gaze darting around the kitchen. "I've been here for two hours and haven't seen another soul."

There was an edge to her voice, like being here alone with me was the worst possible thing. Maybe it was.

I glanced at the windows on either side of the door, the gargoyles now gone, piles of snow in their place. "Maybe they've tried but can't get in because of the snow . . ." I trailed off, a feeling of foreboding overtaking me. "I'm going to check outside."

She didn't say anything as I walked down the set of stairs and toward the door. I attempted to open it, but it wouldn't budge. I yanked at it again, rattling the handle with growing frustration.

"What are you doing?" Elowyn stomped to the top of the stairs. "Just open the door."

"I can't," I said, and this time I was the one with an edge to my voice. As if I hadn't been trying to do that for a full minute now.

"Are you telling me that that door, the only way out of this kitchen, is stuck?" Her last word came out as a squeak.

I yanked again, but the door didn't give at all. It was iced shut. Fuck.

"Oh no." Elowyn shouldered past me, shoving me backward.

"What are you doing?" I asked as she waved a knife and jammed it in the crack between the door and the frame.

"I'm getting us out of here." Her hands shook as she wedged the knife deeper while tugging at the door handle. "There is no way I'm going to be stuck in this kitchen. What if we have to be here all night?"

I hadn't even thought that far ahead, but her words propelled me forward, and I grabbed the handle as well, my hand brushing hers.

She snatched it away.

"Just try and break the ice with that knife while I pull," I instructed.

She gave a curt nod. The door creaked and moaned as she jammed the knife further in the crevice while I pulled that damn handle with all my might.

"I don't think it's working," she panted.

"Come on, come on, come on." I gripped the handle so tight my hands had turned white, and finally, it gave way.

The door swung open, propelling us backward onto the stairs, and once again, Elowyn somehow landed on top of me, except this time, it was her ass grinding right into my crotch, which conjured a lot of really confusing feelings in my body.

Elowyn didn't even notice as she sat up on my lap, her attention focused straight ahead. "Oh, godwitches be."

I only half heard her while my brain was trying to tell my body to calm the fuck down. To remind my cock that we hated her, and this was a completely inappropriate reaction to her sitting on me.

"We're stuck," Elowyn said, voice trembling.

My mouth dropped open as I gathered my wits and joined Elowyn in our current reality. Waves of frigid air blew into the kitchen, and Elowyn shivered.

A solid wall of snow blocked the door, the tips of the gargoyles's horns sticking out from the top.

"No." Elowyn jumped off me and rushed forward, plunging her hands into the snow and digging.

"Elowyn," I said, annoyance flaring. Surely she understood there was no way out of this situation. The snow was too high, too deep, and it was still falling. Knowing her, she'd dig all day, burrow herself in there, and then the snow would bury her alive.

That actually wasn't a bad thought, but I needed her help to get this feast made, and all she was managing to do was let the wintery chill in.

"Elowyn," I said again, but she ignored me. "For fuck's sake," I muttered, stomping forward and grabbing her arm, whirling her to face me.

Her green eyes were wild, her icy, wet hands pressed against my chest. She gripped my apron. "This cannot be happening."

"Well it is." I removed her hands and shoved the door closed. The mop swept past me, sopping up the already melting snow.

Elowyn walked up the stairs and toward the island, She sank against the counter, staring at the door. I followed, waving my hand in front of her face, but she didn't even blink.

"I know this isn't ideal," I said. "But we're in a warm, safe place with plenty of food and water, and we have a lot of work to do."

She swallowed thickly. "Snowed in. We're snowed in."

Elowyn was usually an unstoppable force of nature, much like the unrelenting snow outside. She never took anything too seriously, and I couldn't help but be surprised by her reaction to this.

Maybe she needed some time, so I'd give it to her while I got to work.

I gathered my to-do lists, rifling through the different pages and making notes with my quill. Now that we didn't have the servants helping us, I'd need to adjust a lot of schedules, but if we worked together, we might be able to pull this off.

"What are you doing?" Elowyn snapped.

"Making plans." I crossed one of the items off the list. We'd need to make less dishes, but if we made more of the same dish with a few small variations, then we could batch cook a lot of this food.

She leaned over my shoulder, her scent like cinnamon and cloves, warm and comforting, something I'd never considered Elowyn to be. "How do you do that?" she asked.

"Do what?" I crossed out another item, then scribbled a few ideas next to the line with mashed potatoes. We could definitely do a variety of potato dishes.

"Organize everything, make it all look neat and simple. Your brain has always scared me."

"I could say the same about you," I muttered, thinking of all the times in school that Elowyn would just blurt out an answer to a question, not thinking it through or weighing her options. Yet somehow, her answers were always brilliant, sounding effortless and intelligent in a way I never felt.

Even if her answers had sounded ridiculous, I doubted Elowyn would care. She didn't care what anyone thought of her, me included.

I straightened, tapping the quill on the counter. "If we're going to pull this off, we have to be able to communicate."

She bit the inside of her cheek.

"I know you don't want to screw up the Winter Solstice feast any more than I do, and we're out of buffers. We can't have our own sides of the kitchen or speak through the servants. We're going to have to do this. Together."

She opened her mouth to respond when a screech split the air, and my head whipped toward the dumbwaiter.

"What was that?"

"Elowyn!" a frantic voice called. "Elowyn, are you down there?"

Elowyn's face went pale. "That would be Nan."

"Out of my way, woman," a gruff voice said.

And there was my father.

This day just went from bad to worse.

Six

Liam's face paled, and I imagined he looked how I felt.

"Get your bony elbows out of my ribs," Eamon snapped.

"Make me," Nan said, and I could just imagine the way she was planting her hands on her thin hips and glaring up at him, chin jutting out and everything.

"You think I won't?" he growled back.

"Everything is fine!" Liam called up the dumbwaiter. "Please, for the love of godwitches, do not hit Ms. Carragh."

I swallowed, surprised by the panic in Liam's voice, the worry. I expected him to be like all his bloodthirsty ancestors, who had no qualms with attacking any member of the Carragh family, no matter their gender or age. It was the same with my family. It was a well-known fact that my great-great uncle got into a fist fight with one of Liam's distant female cousins, who actually ended up winning the fight and beating my uncle to a pulp. Not that I condoned that kind of violence, and thankfully, nothing like that had ever happened while I was alive . . . until now.

"Where's Elowyn?" Nan shouted. "Why isn't she speaking? Do you have her tied up?"

Oh, godwitches. My cheeks burned as I imagined Liam tying me up, and the image was horrifying sexual.

I almost snorted out loud. Liam would never tie me up to the bed. He was way too by the book.

"Are you going to say something?" Liam whispered, his eyes bulging.

I ran to the dumbwaiter, realizing I'd been so lost in my thoughts, Nan was now having a full-on meltdown. "If you've hurt my grand-daughter, I'll castrate you and your father!"

Nan loved to threaten castration, even though I was fairly certain it was illegal.

"I'm here!" I burst out. "And I'm fine, Nan. We're both fine, so can the two of you stop fighting?"

"You're fine?" Nan screeched. "You're alone with Liam Wolvern."

"Yes, I'm aware." I leaned in so I could better hear her. "What are you both doing here?"

"I'm not answering that," Liam's father said.

Of course he wouldn't deign to answer a question from a lowly Carragh.

Liam shoved a hand through his hair, something he always did when he was frustrated. I'd noticed it when we were little. Throughout the years, the little quirk of his stuck with me because of how his hair would fall so perfectly in place, framing those high cheekbones and large fore-head, perfectly aligning with his dark brown eyes that popped against his golden skin.

"Father." Liam leaned forward now, both our heads crammed near the opening of the dumbwaiter. "What are you doing here?"

"Well, I—Hey!"

"Elowyn asked me first," Nan snapped.

It was like they were children. Godwitches be, I hoped we never acted like this when Liam and I were their age.

"I saw the snow falling." Nan's voice shook. "And I was worried about a storm, so I came to the castle to bring you some extra layers for your walk home."

"I came to see how everything was going," Eamon said.

"Prince Cillian offered to give us rooms here," Nan said. "So you don't worry about me. You just keep yourself safe. And do not accept any food or beverages from him."

"Seriously?" Liam muttered.

"And, son, don't turn your back on her for a minute, and don't give her any sharp objects."

"She has excellent aim," Nan said menacingly.

"I'm not going to stab him." I pinched the bridge of my nose.

"And I have no plans on poisoning her and being imprisoned for the rest of my life. You two do remember murder is illegal in Fairwitch?"

"That never stopped anyone in the past," Nan said. "And I wouldn't put it past your boy, especially if he's anything like you."

Eamon let out a harsh laugh. "Oh that's rich coming from you."

I turned my head to look at Liam, and he met my gaze, our faces impossibly close, so close I could see the faintest freckles dotting his nose, the little mole right under his left eye. How his eyes reminded me of the deep brown color of my favorite cutting board that I'd gotten for my sixth birthday.

"We have to work together," he said in a low voice. "If they think anything is amiss, they won't leave us alone for a second, and do you want my father and your grandmother shouting at each other for however long we're stuck in here?"

No, no I didn't. It would be a huge distraction, not to mention, downright annoying. Also, I was worried Nan would do something impulsive like shove Eamon down the stairs. I didn't want her to be hauled off to the dungeons.

"Okay," I agreed. "Let's make sure they know everything is fine."

Nan and Eamon were still bickering while we whispered.

"Back up," Nan said. "Your breath smells like death."

"I guess you would know, being so close to death yourself. What are you, now, one hundred?"

"I'm only eighty years old," Nan shot back.

"Excuse me?" I called, wondering what I'd be able to say to convince them to back off. "We're fine. Everything is fine. You two can go to your rooms and relax."

"That sounds like something someone who is not fine would say," Nan shouted.

"I agree," Eamon said.

I let out a sigh and looked at Liam, who just shrugged. "I don't know what they're going to believe. I need to think about this, come up with a plan."

We didn't have time for that. We had a feast to prepare and relatives to get rid of.

I chewed the inside of my cheek, thinking through what might convince Nan, what angle I could use that would persuade her to back off while also persuading Eamon. What did they both want? I snapped my fingers, motioning for Liam to play along.

Well, actually it wouldn't be playing along. This was the truth.

"Nan, listen to me. Liam and I have an entire feast to prepare for the Winter Solstice, and that means we have to work together. Since we're snowed in, we have no one to help us. If we don't pull this off, we'll disappoint the high prince. We'll disappoint the entire city. You know how important Winter Solstice is for everyone."

"It won't just be the city we're disappointing," Liam added. "It'll be the godwitches we're disappointing too."

The entire point of Winter Solstice was to honor the godwitches by coming together and celebrating them and the magic they imparted on our world, by showing our thanks for that magic and each other.

"I would hate to dishonor the food and wine godwitch by ruining this meal. I'd hate to suffer their wrath, to see all our future meals spoiled because we did them a disservice."

Oh, that was good. That was really good. As cooks, the food and wine godwitch was the one we most worshipped and gave thanks to. Many speculated that if a godwitch was displeased, they would show you by making their magic do bad things. For the food and wine godwitch, that could mean food rotting, mysterious foodborne illnesses, and so much more.

Silence descended upon us, and I held my breath, waiting for Nan's response.

"Fine," she said. "If you think you're safe, I suppose I could retire for the evening. There was a large bath chamber with a bathtub as big as my closet, and it is calling my name."

Eamon snorted.

"Father?" Liam asked.

A heavy sigh punctured the silence. "I'll leave you to it, then. But I'll be checking in tomorrow if we're still stuck here."

"Me too!" called Nan. "I'll see you soon, Elowyn, and remember, the groin is a man's most sensitive area."

I rolled my eyes, listening to their footsteps pattering away.

Finally, I slumped against the wall.

"That was good thinking," Liam said quietly. "The only thing they might care about more than hurting each other is dishonoring our patron godwitch."

Both our gazes went to the little statue of the food and wine godwitch sitting on the wooden counter right underneath the window. The godwitch held a butcher knife in one hand and a spatula in the other. They wore a tall chef's hat and apron, and like all the statues of the godwitches, a little wooden offering bowl stood in front of it, filled with coins and dried flowers and herbs. Offerings that reminded the godwitches we worshipped them and thanked them for their magic.

"You think good on your feet," Liam said. "I need time to write things down, to ruminate and reflect. It doesn't always work well in fast-paced environments like this."

I wondered if he was admitting something, if that was the reason why Prince Cillian had wanted me here—because Liam struggled in this kitchen. But no. Liam didn't struggle with anything. He was the golden boy, always doing everything perfectly. It was wishful thinking on my part that he had some weakness I could exploit. At this point, we just needed to survive the feast, and then I could worry about bringing Liam Wolvern down.

I turned to him. "Well, we got rid of them. So what now?"

Seven

LIAM

The sun sank in the sky, and the snow had finally slowed to a few falling flakes instead of a downpour. Half the large stained-glass window was blocked, giving a peek of the beautiful dusty-orange sky, stars already twinkling after the clouds had parted.

Maybe it would warm up tomorrow, and the snow would melt, but for now, it was clear that we'd be here for the night. Temperatures would only continue to drop.

Five balls of dough sat in front of Elowyn. She wiped her glistening forehead with the back of her arm, the sleeves of her dress now rolled up, flour dusting her clothes and apron. A bowl sat in front of her and she massaged the dough with her hands.

I looked down at my chopping board, where I'd chopped handfuls of herbs, all of them being prepared to get mixed into the doughs so we had different varieties.

"We can probably stop soon," I said, nodding toward the sinking sun. "Have something to eat, and then get some sleep."

Elowyn continued to mix the dough with her hands. "For a magical kitchen, it doesn't do a whole lot."

The rhythmic thwack of my knife punctuated her words. "What do you mean?" I asked, deftly chopping the basil in front of me.

"I've always heard about this magical, sentient castle. I've seen its magic with the bickering gargoyles, and I've even seen it shift once, but since I've been in this kitchen. I've barely witnessed any of its magic. Why doesn't it chop and mix and bake? This all would be so much easier if the castle stepped in and helped." She looked up at the ceiling, glaring at it.

"The magic here isn't predictable. Sometimes it does help." I thought of the fire in the hearth, how it sprang to life on its own, no wood needed.

Maybe Elowyn hadn't noticed.

"Sometimes the knives will chop on their own. Sometimes I have to do it. Sometimes pots and pans will float through the air and land right where I need them. Other times"—I shrugged—"not so much."

"I guess we're in the 'not so much' phase right now," she muttered. "And my hands are killing me. I could really use some magic," she called out.

"Don't test the castle," I said. "It's been known to get grumpy."

She let out a disbelieving laugh. "The castle gets grumpy?"

"Yeah." I turned back to my cutting board, sliding my pile of basil over to make room for some sun-dried tomatoes I'd found in the pantry, deciding to put them together into one of the loaves. It had actually been Elowyn's idea, and I figured we could try it out, so I'd written out the recipe and handed it over.

I'd chop. She'd mix. Then we'd let the dough sit in the icebox, where it would slowly rise over the next few days.

"One time," I said over my shoulder, "one of the servants complained that the fire was too hot, and an ember flew right onto her skirt. She had to stop, drop, and roll, but her entire skirt got burned off in the process so everyone got a nice glimpse of her undergarments."

Elowyn laughed, the sound so light and airy, so her. I'd heard her laugh many times over the years but never because of something I'd said, and I got this urge to make her do it again.

I turned, wanting to see what she looked like when she laughed, how her face might be lit up, how her eyes might be dancing, the curve of her smile . . . but the smile on my face quickly died. Elowyn shoved her hands in her apron pockets, giving me a bright smile that didn't reach her eyes.

"What are you doing?" I asked, gaze narrowing.

"Nothing," she squeaked. I'd seen the guilty look on her face hundreds of times before. When she was caught sneaking a note to a classmate. When she was caught cheating off my paper. When she told Greta Ferg her new haircut looked nice.

I wiped my hands on my apron and stalked toward her as she backed up against the counter, hands braced against the edge.

I slowly slipped my hands into the front pockets of her apron.

"Excuse you!" she yelled, but she had nowhere to go, not with me hovering so close.

I pulled out two vials of seeds, eyes widening in horror as I noticed my crumpled recipes scattered across the counter. She hadn't even read them.

"What is this?" I held up the vials.

"Just some sesame and poppy seeds."

Black seeds peppered the dough in her mixing bowl.

"Why would you add these? This recipe is supposed to be onion, salt, and garlic."

"I just thought these might make a great addition. I found them in the pantry when I was getting more flour, and the idea just popped in my head."

My temple was pounding. "The idea popped in your head?" I asked. "What if adding the seeds changes the consistency, changes the baking time, changes how the flavors react? What if it ruins the entire loaf?"

"What if it doesn't?" She raised her chin stubbornly. "What if it's the best thing you've ever tasted?"

I groaned. "You didn't mean it. Not any of it." Godwitches be, this was so fucking typical of Elowyn. She didn't care about anybody but herself. Only wanted to hear her own ideas. Only wanted to work alone . . . unless of course she didn't do the group assignment and then she wanted me to do all the work while she got the excellent marks from the teacher.

"Didn't mean what?" She blew a stray strand of hair from her forehead.

"What you said to your nan and my father. You don't want to work together. You want to sweep in here and change everything to your liking, hoping maybe you'll impress the high prince and take my job. Right?"

She bit her lip.

"I fucking knew it." I slammed the vials on either side of her, my face inches from hers. "Well, I'm not letting you. I'm still chef of this kitchen, and I say no."

Her eyebrows flew up as I grabbed the bowl of dough.

"What are you doing?" she asked as I stalked toward the door.

"Throwing this out."

"Don't you dare. I worked hard on that. The least we can do is bake it and—"

I stomped down the stairs and wrenched the door open, and a blast of wintry air barreled past me.

"Stop!" She grabbed the bowl and I whirled to face her while I gripped the other side.

"This is impossible," I yelled over the sound of the wind and snow. "We can't work together. We've never been able to."

She yanked it toward her. "What does that mean?"

I heaved it backward toward my stomach, forcing her to take a few steps forward. "Back in school," I said. "Nothing has changed. We couldn't work together then and we can't work together now."

She gave a disbelieving laugh. "That was over a decade ago. And you're still judging me. You're still watching every move I make with disapproval like you always have."

Her accusation made my hackles rise. "What else am I supposed to do? Be happy that you can never follow the rules, that you just have to do things your own way, leaving carnage trailing behind wherever you go."

Her mouth dropped open, eyes going glassy, and I regretted my words instantly. She sniffled, and I thought she was about to let the bowl go, but instead, her face sank back into a determined scowl as she lifted her foot and stomped down on mine.

Pain shot through my foot right as another gust of snow-filled wind blew into the kitchen. I lost my footing and stumbled forward into Elowyn, my face going straight into the mixing bowl. She shrieked and jumped back, letting go of the bowl that my face was planted into, and down I went. My body slammed against the stairs, knees jolting in pain while sticky dough coated my cheeks, my nose, my eyes. It was everywhere.

Elowyn shrieked somewhere nearby, and I lifted my head, trying to see through the sticky mess covering my eyes. Off-white powder swirled through the air, coating everything in the kitchen, and I wondered if it was snow. Goosebumps pebbled my entire body as the wind continued to batter our kitchen, nipping at all my exposed flesh.

I sat up, head dizzy, nose filled with the scent of yeast. I wiped blobs of dough out of my eyes, realizing Elowyn had gone up the stairs and tripped over a sack of flour. It had exploded and was now being blown everywhere by the icy wind.

Godwitches be, it was cold.

"Ow." Elowyn lay on her back, completely covered in flour, staring up at the ceiling, and I scrambled to shut the door, which wasn't easy when I was fighting against a snowstorm. It finally slammed closed, the howling wind dying into the background.

I had been so naive to ever think we could do this. The hatred between our two families was too deep.

"I think I might have died by flour suffocation," Elowyn said weakly from the floor. "Am I dead? Have I gone to the Otherworld to be greeted and welcomed by the godwitches?"

"I doubt they'd be welcoming you," I muttered and stomped up the stairs, standing over her.

I licked my lips, getting a taste of something absolutely delicious. It was savory, the salty flavors bursting on my tongue. I loomed over Elowyn, realizing what I was tasting: her creation. This was what I'd fought her over.

And it was fucking delightful.

Eight

ELOWYN

I sat up, head throbbing from hitting it on the ground, and gaped. My body looked like a snowflake. Flour covered every inch of me, and I slowly sat up to see Liam, whose face was covered in my dough, laughing.

Liam Wolvern was laughing. I wasn't sure I'd ever seen him laugh—he was always so serious, so focused.

He pointed. "You have a little something."

My fingers went to my cheek, and then I realized he was joking. He'd just made an actual joke.

I stared at the dough on his face, little black seeds peppering it. "So do you." My lips twitched, and before I could help it, I was laughing along with him.

Forget poison and knives. We'd suffer death by cooking, suffocating in flour and dough. It was ridiculous. This whole thing was ridiculous. A stupid family rivalry because supposedly one of my ancestors stole a recipe from his—or his stole a recipe from mine. It had been so long ago, no one was even sure what the truth was anymore.

We just hated each other because we were supposed to, and right now, that hatred was ruining this entire experience. I'd waited my whole life to step into the castle kitchen, to be able to cook in here, and instead of savoring these moments, I was spending them bickering with Liam like we were still children.

His laughter had died as he stared down at me, brown eyes swirling with emotion.

"I was never judging you, you know," he said, wiping some of the dough off his face.

"W-what?" I asked.

He shoved a hand through his hair, which only further spread the dough. "You said I'm judging like I always do. I've never judged you, Elowyn, though I get why you think I have."

My mouth dropped open, and my instinct was to not believe him. "But you were always glaring at me whenever I arrived late to school or was doodling in my notebook instead of taking notes. You were always telling me I was doing things wrong."

"Because I was jealous. I still am, if we're being honest."

I froze, unable to understand what he was telling me. Liam Perfect Wolvern was jealous of me? It didn't seem possible.

"Why would you be jealous of me?" I asked. "You're the one who got this job."

"And I'm failing at it," he said, voice strained. "That's why you're here. Because I'm clearly not fit to be the castle chef."

None of this was making sense, and I waited for Liam to explain.

"Everything comes so easy to you," he said. "Despite missing half our classes, constantly coming in late, never taking notes, you breezed through it all. You can think on your feet, improvise, and you do it with this air of confidence and calm. You didn't even bat an eye before adding new ingredients to my dough recipe. Do you know how long it would've taken me to change a recipe? I would've had to think about it for a week, then make a comprehensive pros and cons list. I would've had to bake my original recipe, then bake my new recipe, then get about a million opinions on it, and I still would've felt sick at the thought of trying something that could turn out bad. You just did it." He licked his bottom lip. "And it's fucking delicious."

I let out a laugh but had a fleeting thought that I'd entered some upside-down world with an upside-down Liam.

"But you're perfect" was all I could manage, and Liam gave a harsh laugh.

"That's what you think?"

"Of course it is." I spread out my arms. "You have everything so together. You're so organized. You make lists and plans, and they're good ones. It's not your fault I changed the recipe." I bit my lip, cracks forming in the armor I put up whenever I was around Liam. "I can't help it. Your recipe was good. I just . . . sometimes I have a hard time concentrating unless I'm trying something new. It was the same way in school. I didn't take notes because it was hard to keep my brain on task, to do the same routine day in and day out. I was late because I'd get so distracted on the way to school with about a million different things. Trees, bugs, people. I still have those problems. Despite living in the apartment over the Deerborn, I still manage to be late to my shifts."

Behind all the dough, his eyes widened, and I could tell he was as surprised by my admission as I'd been by his.

"I always thought you just didn't care."

I shrugged. "And I always thought you were an asshole."

He laughed. "What about now?"

I studied him. "Now I think it's very hard to take you seriously with all that dough covering your face."

He burst out laughing again, and it was the most refreshing thing I'd heard in a long time.

Nine

ELOWYN

Hours later, we'd managed to get the kitchen—and ourselves—cleaned. Except my hair, flour still tangled in the strands.

A barrel brimming with water sat in the corner at the edge of the counter, and I eyed it, debating just how badly I wanted to get clean. On the one hand, it would be great to not have flour in my hair. On the other hand, despite the sweat coating my skin after hours of scrubbing, dusting, and sweeping, I was already cold and washing my hair would only make me feel colder.

Liam finished polishing the last bit of counter that flour covered and turned, yawning and stretching his arms up, revealing a shock of golden skin just above the waistband of his trousers, and an unholy image of me licking that strip of skin flashed through my brain.

My gaze snapped to meet his, and I gave him a weak smile, praying to the godwitches he hadn't just seen me gawking. We might've made somewhat of a truce with our earlier admissions, but that didn't mean I could start ogling him. Liam was an objectively attractive person. He had golden skin and blonde hair, a strong square jaw, was intelligent, an amazing cook, and had always been known in Fairwitch as being polite and respectful—basically he was the full package. I was actually surprised he wasn't courting anyone.

Or maybe he was. It wasn't like I was privy to the personal details of his life. And I didn't want to be. We were allies in this kitchen, but we could never be actual friends . . .

"Are you okay?"

I startled, looking at him. "Huh?"

"You're pacing." He pointed, and I stopped, realizing he was right, that I'd been walking back and forth, chewing my thumbnail while I spiraled into my thoughts.

"My hair is dirty," I blurted out, not sure what else to say.

"Yes." Liam crossed his arms, and for the first time ever, I noticed the rippling muscles underneath his shirt.

Godwitches be, get it together Elowyn. One semi-sappy moment between us and all of a sudden, I was increasingly aware of how attractive Liam Wolvern was, and just thinking that felt like a huge betrayal to my family.

When we were bonding, it felt necessary to achieve our common goal, to make the godwitch of food and wine proud. To give our city a Winter Solstice Feast to remember. But there was absolutely no justification for anything further developing between us.

"You're pacing again," Liam pointed out.

I stopped. "I'm really stressed . . . about my hair."

"I can help you clean it," Liam offered. "Since it's half my fault you got it dirty in the first place."

"No," I squeaked, mind already in enough of a panic. The last thing I needed was him massaging my scalp.

"Here." He crouched down and grabbed an empty wooden bucket off one of the lower shelves underneath the counter, then stood and held it out to me.

I grabbed it, dipping it into the barrel of water.

I turned to see Liam with a rag and a bar of soap. "This should do the trick."

I heaved the heavy bucket up onto the island and accepted the rag and soap, staring at them both like I had no idea what to do. I really missed my bath chamber right now, the water Mama would pour into it after heating it over the hearth fire and how I'd soak after a long day at the tavern.

Dread filled me at the bucket of cold water sitting there. I steeled myself and dipped my head in. Icy water shocked my scalp, a thousand little cuts pricking my head. I lifted my sopping hair from the bucket, drops of the cold water flinging all over, trickling down my back like a knife dragging over my skin.

I grimaced, reaching for the bar when Liam grabbed my hand.

"What are you doing?" I asked with chattering teeth.

"Listen," Liam said. "It's going to be hard to do this yourself with a tiny bucket of water, so just let me help. I can wash your hair. I've done it for my little sister a thousand times."

I squeezed my eyes shut, bones frozen and weary. I was too tired to argue, so I just nodded, letting Liam take over.

He grabbed a chair and put it against a smaller table next to the water barrel. I watched as he methodically moved everything over to the table, including a small cup. He grabbed the dry rag and wrapped my hair in it.

My hands went up over my head to keep it in place.

"Go on." He gestured to the table. "Sit in the chair."

I hesitated only for a moment, then sank down and leaned my head back over the bucket. I had to admit, this was a much better idea than mine, which had been to just plunge my head right in and send my body into shock.

I closed my eyes and heard the quiet dip of the cup into the bucket, then gasped as Liam poured the water over my head.

"Sorry," he said, and he sounded genuinely apologetic that I was so uncomfortable.

Then his fingers dug into my scalp, and all the cold was replaced by warmth, his warmth. He kneaded my skin gently, lulling me, the tension bleeding from my shoulders. No one had washed my hair since I was little, and it felt surprisingly good, even more surprising that this kind of tenderness and care came from Liam. He'd always seemed so rigid in everything he did. But this was not remotely rigid.

"Are you okay?" he asked.

"Mm-hmm," I managed. "You're really good at this. Do you massage scalps regularly?"

He laughed, the sound rumbling right down to my belly. "I told you. I used to wash my sister's hair when she was younger. After our mother died, I took care of her a lot. My father was always busy at the bakery."

I'd known this. I'd known Liam's mother died, and I'd known he had to take care of his little sister. I used to feel so sorry for his sister, wondering if I could smuggle her out of the Wolvern family, and now . . . well, now I was seeing this entirely different side of Liam that I'd never expected. It had happened in a matter of hours, and it had somehow turned my entire worldview on its head.

"I'm sorry about your mother," I said.

She'd died, along with Liam's grandparents, during an attack on Fairwitch. Some magical creature had gotten in, despite the barriers that made our city invisible, and it had ripped them all to shreds. Fairwitch was hidden for a reason—our sentient castle was a valuable piece of magic that many would love to conquer. But the castle's magic kept us hidden, mostly safe—except from other magical creatures or objects, which could infiltrate the barrier. The attacks had been getting worse, and at this point, we feared someone had discovered us, that they couldn't get into our city, so instead, they were sending magical weapons in to weaken us.

Liam's mother had died far too young. We'd been barely teenagers. Despite the family rivalry, that had been the one time we'd reached out to the Wolverns, gifting them with food—the only way we knew to show love. They'd never responded, or thanked us, and we hadn't expected them to or begrudged them. They were suffering beyond the imaginable.

But as time wore on and the Wolverns reemerged into society, the rivalry picked back up, just like it always had.

"Thank you," Liam said. "Sometimes, I think . . ."

He trailed off, his fingers still massaging my scalp, and with each dig of his fingertips, my body sank deeper into that chair and my eyes grew a little heavier.

"Sometimes you think what?" I asked.

"My mother was like me. She had lists for her lists. She understood me in a way my father never has, and I don't even care anymore that my father doesn't see the real me—I'm thirty years old, and I abandoned the hope long ago that he'd ever accept me for who I am."

I wanted to ask who that was, not entirely following.

"But I do care about how it will affect Ava. I need this position because if I lose it, all that pressure will fall to Ava's shoulders. She'll be the one expected to somehow get the castle chef position. He won't let her have a life. A future. At least not one she wants for herself."

I was so tired, and his fingers felt so good. Too good. I wanted to ask him what he wanted for himself. If he was trying to tell me he didn't want to be a chef, then what did he want to be? I couldn't imagine Liam not cooking. He was too good, had too much talent to belong anywhere other than a kitchen. But all those thoughts slowly faded as I drifted to sleep under Liam's touch.

Ten

LIAM

Washing Elowyn's hair had been a mistake.

Washing Ava's hair had always felt like a parental duty. I'd never particularly enjoyed it, mainly because bathing my sister when she was small was the equivalent of trying to bathe a wild cat.

Washing Elowyn's hair was nothing like that. She writhed under my fingers, her hips arching, and moans escaping her mouth that shot straight to my fucking cock. I knew she was asleep, that this was all happening somewhere deep inside her brain, something she'd likely not even remember, but I'd never forget it.

She let out another deep moan as I scrubbed soap into her hair, trying to get all the flour out of her dark strands. That moan would be imprinted on me until the day I died. It made me wonder what other things I could do to get her to make a sound like that, and that's when I snatched my hands away and poured cold water right over her head.

She jolted awake, sitting straight up in her chair, wild-eyed, and confused. "W-what's going on?"

"We're finished." I grabbed the rag and wrapped it around her hair. "All clean."

She slowly turned those big green eyes onto me, and I practically melted under them. Ever since that small moment where we both admitted vulnerabilities, it was like I saw her in this whole new light. Like I could look back on every single past infraction and see it from a different perspective, one where Elowyn wasn't careless or apathetic—but trying to find her own way. She reminded me a lot of Ava. She always had, but whereas I saw Ava as adventurous and brave and innovative, Elowyn had always been colored by my prejudices toward her family. I hadn't lied to her. I'd never judged her, but I had disliked her simply because I was supposed to.

She blinked, toweling off her hair and removing the rag, her wet strands wavy and hanging to her shoulders, droplets clinging to the ends. "Oh, I feel so much better." She shivered. "Godwitches, it's cold in here."

I shivered, too, noticing that it was unusually frigid, probably because we'd left the door open so long during our fight.

"Um, is the fire supposed to be out?" Elowyn pointed a shaking finger toward the hearth.

The very empty hearth.

"No, it's not." I crouched, peering at the glowing orange embers, all that was left the fire. Maybe the wind had blown it out, but why hadn't it started again?

"Can't we just build another one?"

I straightened and turned. "No, we can't. Because the fire is one of the things the castle just does." I snapped my fingers. "Magic. No wood required, no maintenance. When we need a fire, it appears."

"That sounds helpful," Elowyn said.

"It would be. If it was working right now." I glared at the hearth, willing it to spark to life. "I've never even thought about it because it's always just here." Until now.

"What's changed . . ." Elowyn drifted off as if she was realizing exactly what had changed.

She was the only difference in this kitchen. Maybe even though Prince Cillian invited her here, the castle didn't approve. That filled me with hope—and some guilt, but mostly hope. Because if the castle didn't want her, there was nothing Prince Cillian could do. It was the castle who had chosen the high prince to rule when a golden crown had appeared over his head. At the end of the day, everyone in Fairwitch knew who was really in charge.

"Right." Elowyn twisted a wet strand of hair, trembling, water dripping onto her clothes. "What are we going to do without a fire? It's really cold, and I'm getting tired. I also have to . . . relieve myself."

"We do have a chamber pot." I nodded my head toward the pantry. "There's a door in the back of the pantry that leads to the chamber pot. This used to be a groundskeeper's apartment, but it got turned into the castle kitchen a few centuries ago."

"Great. Thank you for the history lesson. I'm just going to . . ." She spun on her heel and made her way toward the pantry, disappearing from view while I frowned at the hearth.

All the warmth I'd felt massaging her head had dried up like water in a desert. Goosebumps now pebbled my skin, and my teeth chattered.

As the night wore on, it was only going to get colder. By this point, everyone else would be asleep; otherwise, I might be tempted yell for someone to throw us some extra cloaks and blankets. I eyed both my and Elowyn's cloaks that hung in the corner, and my stomach sank as a solution came to mind.

She wasn't going to like this.

I didn't like this.

But at this point, it wasn't about being enemies or rivals or tentative colleagues. It was about surviving what would be a very cold night without a fire to keep us warm.

Elowyn reemerged a few minutes later, still shivering and scowling. "Why has your face gone all pale? What's wrong now?"

I stood. "You're not going to like this."

She groaned.

"We don't have a fire."

"Yes, I can see that."

"It's only going to get colder, and you have wet hair." I swallowed thickly. "If we want to survive tonight, we're going to have to sleep together."

"Excuse you?" Her voice rose three octaves.

"For body heat," I said. "I know it's not ideal—"

"Not ideal?" Her eyes had widened to saucers. "Of course it's not ideal."

"But it's going to keep us from getting hypothermia. The castle is not giving us a fire, and I can't build a fire without any wood."

"We're just going to sleep on the stone floor and . . . cuddle?"

I scratched the back of my neck. "I have a bed pallet. There's been a few nights when I've had to sleep here." Because I was so full of anxiety I couldn't go home and face my father, who'd instantly know something was wrong and interrogate me into a full-on panic attack.

"Why would you spend the night here?" Her eyes narrowed.

"Just a lot of work to do," I said quickly. "Wasn't worth trekking home and then coming back in the morning."

She chewed on the inside of her cheek, then huffed. "I suppose we have no other options since the castle's magic suddenly decided to start malfunction right when I arrived—" She stopped suddenly.

"Like I said, the castle's magic is unpredictable. It's probably just a coincidence that it stopped working when you came." I had no idea why I was trying to make her feel better—probably the cold addling my brain.

"Right." She rocked on her heels, looking as awkward as I felt.

I dashed to the bottom shelf under the counter and pulled out my thick bed pallet and blanket, along with a single feather-stuffed pillow. "It's going to be a tight fit."

She flashed a strained smile. "Perfect."

I laid the pallet and pillow in front of the fire in case it roared back to life at some point, then I spread out the blanket and laid down. Elowyn sidled closer, eyeing me like I was a snake that might strike.

She sat next to me in the pallet. "Should I just . . ." She gestured to the small space in front of me.

"Go ahead and lie down," I said.

She didn't say anything, just laid down and molded her body to mine.

Godwitches be. "Can I put my arm around you?"

"Okay." Her voice came out breathy in a way I hadn't expected, flooding me with warmth. I wrapped my arm around her waist as she wiggled against me.

"Can you please not do that?" I asked with a strained voice.

"I'm trying to get comfortable. I'm not used to sleeping with anyone."

"What about Conan?" The question about the man she used to court came out before I could stop it.

She stiffened in my arms. Fuck. Way to make it awkward with the woman I was going to have to sleep next to all night.

"Conan never slept over," she said. "We weren't in an actual relationship. I haven't had many of those." She paused. "Or any."

Oh. I'd seen Elowyn with plenty of men over the years, outside our bakery or picnicking in the green hills or dancing at the various balls throughout the year.

"I like to have fun," Elowyn said.

That made sense and was in line with everything I knew about her. She liked new things, experimenting, adventure. A relationship wouldn't fit well into her life when she was constantly seeking excitement—the opposite of what I wanted.

She wiggled some more, and I winced.

"Sorry," she said quickly. "What about you? Whatever happened with you and Fiona?"

I was surprised she knew about that. Unlike Elowyn, I didn't flit about town with the women I courted. Then again, Fairwitch was small, and gossip spread easily. I'd courted Fiona on and off for years, but we'd decided to end it for good about a year ago.

"She didn't like how much I worked," I said. "And my father didn't like me getting distracted. Even before I got the job here, I was so busy at the bakery. My father always expected work to come first, and then there was the training."

"Training?" she asked.

"Every night after work. He'd test me and train me for this royal chef job. Make me whip up a new dish on the spot, then analyze every place where I'd gone wrong."

"That sounds intense," Elowyn said.

That was a word for it. It was more like torture. I'd had to start running at night after the training sessions. I'd run and run and run until I couldn't anymore, until my body was so tired it would shut down and I could sleep with none of my father's hopes and dreams weighing on me.

"Why did he make you do that?" Elowyn turned around, her face so close to mine I could see the yellow rings around her irises. "You've always been so disciplined, so good at what you do."

That was why I was good at what I did. "My father's a good man. He's given his whole life toward making me the chef I am today. It was always his dream for me to be this. Ever since he lost the role to your aunt."

She stared at me, sympathy flashing in her gaze, and it felt like she could see right through my words, right into the heart of them. It felt like she saw me for maybe the first time ever. She opened her mouth to speak, then closed it, then opened it again. "We should get some sleep," she finally whispered. "We have another long day tomorrow."

She turned around, her body once again pressed tight to mine.

It was going to be a long, long night.

Eleven

ELOWYN

The kitchen was dark, the smell of crisp winter air and burning ash mingling. Even with the chill rattling the windows, I was warm. Not just warm, hot. Deliciously heated.

Liam's hard length pushing into my back, and desire flooded between my legs in response. I wiggled, desperately needing a release, and he let out a moan that made my knees go weak.

I hadn't been with a man in months, but why had my body chosen this moment to want one between my legs? To want *him*?

Maybe it was his closeness, the way he smelled like freshly baked bread and ash; maybe it was the hard edges and stiff ridges of his muscles or the way his arm cradled me; maybe it was his warm breath puffing on my neck, making the hairs raise.

Whatever it was, I had a desperate need to roll over and see what might happen between us.

His hard length stiffened, and some of that self-control I was gripping onto slipped.

My breath caught at how hard he was . . . for me. I was wide awake now, all the heat in my body rushing between my legs.

"Do you want this as badly as I do?" he whispered in my ear.

My eyes widened at the realization he wasn't sleeping.

I turned and we stared at each other, the moon's glow painting him blue. I traced the freckles on his face. I'd seen them a million times sitting next to him in class, but this was the first time I'd ever felt the urge to touch them.

He shuddered. "You're going to have to stop that."

"Why?" I asked.

"Because if you don't, the last shred of self control I have will snap."

I continued staring into his dark brown eyes, rich and layered like the oak wood in our tavern. I didn't stop, still tracing the freckles, trailing my finger over his nose like a challenge.

His gaze flashed, pupils blowing out, and his lips pressed gently to mine. The kiss started slow, but soon the tension between us snapped, our mouths devouring each other, lips and tongues tangling wildly, hands roaming with abandon.

Abruptly he gripped my hips and flipped me so that my back was once again pressed to his chest, and he leaned down, whispering in my ear, "I want you to rub yourself against me again."

I whimpered, used to this bossy Liam, normally hating his superior "I know best" tone, but this time, it didn't bother me. I wanted to listen.

I arched my back and rocked against him, loving the feel of his hard body.

"Now touch yourself," he said. "I know you're wet for me. I felt it just a moment ago."

At his command, my hands slid down to my clit, and I rubbed in slow circles, continuing to rock against him, increasing my pace as he kissed my neck, his lips so warm and soft, his kisses building that fire already sparking inside of me.

"Oh, godwitches," I said as another moan escaped my mouth. Sensations exploded throughout my body, and I was hardly able to summon a thought except that I wanted more.

That whatever was happening between us was just a taste, and there was no way my body would be satiated, not when I'd remember exactly how his hard length pushed into me, the way I needed to know how it would feel between my legs, in my mouth, rubbing circles over my clit.

Now that I was getting this preview of Liam Wolvern, all I wanted was more, more, more.

My fingers circled with increasing intensity while I continued my rhythm, rubbing against Liam as his moans matched mine.

"Elowyn!" a voice called, the sound loud and screechy. I stiffened, my fingers faltering. Nan? What was she doing up in the middle of the night? "Elowyn!" she yelled again. "If you don't answer, I'm stabbing Liam's father."

Liam had stopped moving behind me, his warm breath and lips gone from my neck.

"Elowyn, wake up," Liam said, voice low and urgent.

Wake up? My eyes blinked open, vision blurry, slowly clearing to reveal a sun-lit kitchen and Liam's pinched face hovering over me.

I jolted upright, my head knocking straight into his.

"Ow. Fuck," he said.

"What's going on down there?" his father yelled to my absolute horror.

"Is that boy up to no good?" Nan asked. "I've got my knife ready, Elowyn."

"Fuck that hurt." Liam clutched his nose. "Could you please say something before your Nan kills my father—"

"Here. I'm here," I managed, feeling like someone had just dunked me into an ice bucket.

Just a moment ago, I'd been about to come. I'd been about to make Liam come. It had been pitch black, and . . . none of it had been real.

I'd been dreaming the whole thing. I'd had a sex dream about Liam Wolvern, which was so absurdly inappropriate given our history, our families' history. All it took to have a sex dream about him was a few nice little moments between us? Was I that desperate?

I didn't want to answer that question.

"Are you okay?" Liam asked, staring at me. "You look a little flushed."

"Why is she flushed?" Nan shouted. "Are you sick? Did he cough in your face or something?"

No, he did other things to my body. Things that weren't real because my mind had decided to make them up.

"W-what?" Liam sputtered toward the dumbwaiter. "No, I didn't cough in her face. And I'm not even sick."

"Son, don't feel obligated to respond to the ramblings of a crazy woman."

"Thank you," Nan said, sounding flattered by the description instead of insulted.

I managed to stand, legs wobbly and area between my legs sore like I'd had a wild night of passion, but no, I just had all the effects of it without any actual fun. I felt raw and utterly confused.

I swallowed thickly, my gaze straying to the window, snow covering half of it.

We were still stuck in here, and I wasn't sure I could handle any more of Liam holding me. I might explode if I had another dream like the one I'd had last night.

"Elowyn," Nan snapped.

"Hm?" I looked in the direction of the dumbwaiter.

"Your nan was asking if you needed her to drop you a butcher knife," Liam said, hair tousled and wavy and golden under the sun shining through the tops of the windows.

"No, Nan. I've got plenty of knives already if I'm in a stabbing mood."

Liam shot me an alarmed look.

"That's my girl," Nan said. "Remember what I taught you with that jab and twist move."

Liam's eyes widened even further, his skin losing some of its color.

"How are preparations for the feast coming?" Liam's father asked, apparently not remotely concerned about the possibility of me stabbing his son.

"Good," we both said at the same time despite the fact that we'd gotten absolutely nothing done after the disaster that was yesterday.

"Speaking of the feast," Liam said. "It's in six days." He frowned. "Or it should be if this snow ever melts. So we really need to get cooking."

"Is she distracting you?" his father barked.

Liam crossed his arms. "I am capable of cooking with a few distractions."

For some stupid reason, it stung that he didn't defend me, didn't stand up to his father and tell him we were actually getting along. Then again, I hadn't said anything to Nan. Mainly because then Nan would think I was being tied up and tortured, and she'd probably try to shimmy down the dumbwaiter to rescue me.

"Good because you cannot afford any distractions," Eamon said.

Liam's eyes rolled upward. "I'm aware, Father."

"This feast needs to be perfect. Impeccable. The best you've ever cooked. Do what I couldn't do, son. Make me proud."

I might've imagined it, but I could've sworn I saw the slightest shake to Liam's hands as he grabbed one of the mixing bowls we'd cleaned last night.

"It will be the best with my Elowyn helping." Pride filled Nan's voice, and Liam's jaw locked.

"Okay," I said. "That's enough out of both of you. We need to concentrate, so please go away and do not go anywhere near each other today."

Grumbles met my comment, but footsteps echoed, pattering away and leaving me and Liam alone.

With the distraction gone, all thoughts of my dream about Liam came rushing back, along with the awareness that we were very, very alone. My skin itched with heat as he came closer, and I jumped back.

"Are you okay?" His eyebrows bunched.

"Mm-hm." I leaned down taking a big scoop of flour and dumping it in my bowl.

He shivered, and I realized our breaths were puffing from our mouths, but I hadn't even noticed because I was so heated from . . . other things.

Right then, the fire burst to life in the hearth, the warmth glorious against my chilled skin.

"Seriously?" I asked the castle. "Now? You choose now to come back?"

Liam put a finger to his mouth. "Let's not anger the castle after it just gave us fire."

If it had given us the fire last night, all this could've been avoided. The bonding, the weird feelings that came after, the even weirder dream that I couldn't get out of my mind.

At least with the fire, we could avoid cuddling tonight. And that was the only thought that could got me through the rest of the day.

Twelve

LIAM

Three days. Three days of being snowed in with Elowyn. At least we'd gotten our fire back, no longer having to cuddle at night.

Thank the godwitches because that night cradling her in my arms had been the longest of my life. I'd barely slept; every time Elowyn moved, she'd rubbed against my fucking cock, giving me a hard-on that I couldn't even relieve. I'd just had to lay there and count sheep and think of my late grandmother and recite prayers to the godwitches we'd all had to memorize in school.

None of it worked.

Then Elowyn had started moaning. Moaning my name.

Just the memory of it made my cock twitch again, the way she said my name like a plea, like I was withholding something from her, something that she badly wanted.

That right there had almost been enough to make me come, but then she'd started rubbing against me, moving that soft ass in a torturous rhythm. I'd tried to shift, but she reached back and grabbed my arm with a tight grip. Also, there wasn't really anywhere to go with both of us tucked into the bedroll.

I'd thought about waking her up, but I always heard you shouldn't wake someone from a dream. So I'd just let her keep going while I sweated through my clothes, thinking about the most unattractive things I could: dough that didn't rise, my father lecturing me, blood gushing from my hand after I'd cut myself with a knife.

I deserved a damn medal for the way I'd kept my body from responding.

Because if she'd been awake and aware, there was absolutely nothing in the world that would've stopped me from grabbing her hips and flipping her over so she could properly ride me, so I could make her come and hear more of those delicious sounds coming from her, hear my name on her lips as my cock filled her.

"Is the squash done?" Elowyn asked, and I looked up from where I was sprinkling it with sugar, getting it ready to caramelize and go into a savory spinach, cheese, and egg quiche.

Elowyn stood on the opposite side of the room, working on some kind of whipped butter to dip the bread in. She mashed the butter in a bowl with a spatula.

"Almost," I said, avoiding eye contact.

Elowyn had been distant the last few days, and I had no interest in questioning why. At night, we'd both slept in front of the fire, still sharing my pallet but stuffing the blanket between us as a barrier, and I'd heard no more moans coming from her side.

The problem was, I couldn't tell if I was more frustrated or elated by that fact.

Either way, I needed to focus. The winter feast was four days away, and while we'd made good progress now that we were no longer fighting, we still weren't anywhere close to where we needed to be. I glanced at Elowyn, who was following her own recipe while I worked on mine.

We'd agreed we would split the menu in half, and Elowyn would cook the recipes on her list while I'd cook the ones on mine. If Elowyn wanted to take liberties with hers, I wouldn't stop her. We couldn't afford another fight that ruined all our progress.

"Oh, godwitches." Elowyn held a fist to her mouth, looking a little green.

"What? What is it?"

She grabbed the waste bucket and spit whatever was in her mouth into it. She wiped her lips with the back of her hand and turned so I couldn't see her face.

"Are you okay?" I asked. "Was there something wrong with the butter?"

A soft sob escaped Elowyn, and I stilled, noticing the slightest tremble to her shoulders. She was crying. I'd never seen Elowyn cry, not in all my years of knowing her. She was always bubbly and carefree and fun and, sometimes, fiery. But never sad.

It took just a few long strides, and I was at her side, gently grabbing the crook of her elbow to turn her to me.

"It's just some butter," I said.

She pawed at the tears on her cheeks, and the sight chipped away at all the walls I'd been so good at putting up these last few days.

"I'm jealous of you too," she said, voice so soft I almost didn't hear.

"What?" I asked.

She sniffled. "Don't make me say it again."

I'd heard her. I just couldn't believe it. "Why are you jealous of me?"

She threw up her arms. "Because you're so organized in a way I could never be. You have this ability to know exactly the right steps and right ingredients to make something good." Red rimmed her eyes, the tears turning them a light green. "Sometimes I feel like I'll never be as consistently good as you. Yes, I can make magic with some of my creations." She gestured toward the butter. "But just as many times I ruin dishes. I get too overzealous and it's all wrong." She swallowed. "I think it's my fault the tavern is failing. I like to blame Nan and my parents for refusing to change, but I've changed so many recipes without them knowing, serving customers who didn't end up liking their dish."

My heart cracked at the vulnerability in her voice, at the well of sadness in her eyes.

"At least you're not afraid to try," I said. "My dishes are good like you said. Just good. That dough you made the other day, where you added poppy seeds and sesame seeds? It was amazing. Not just food but an experience." I thumbed away a tear as it rolled down her cheek. "That's something that can't be taught, a gift. And of course you're going to fail sometimes. At least you have the courage to. You're not the reason your tavern is failing. It's the world we live in. These attacks. The weight on our city. You'll bounce back. The Carraghs never quit. Elowyn Carragh never quits."

A small smile tipped the corners of her lips. "I can't believe I'm getting complimented by Liam Wolvern."

I snorted. "I can't believe Elowyn Carragh is jealous of me."

A laugh bubbled out of her, and she shot a sideways glance at the butter. "Maybe we're going about this all wrong."

I arched a brow.

"You are good at organizing and keeping us on track and planning meals. I'm good at creativity, bringing new flavors together. So why don't we actually try and be a team?"

It was a logical suggestion, a good one, even. Except for the problem that just standing next to her, inhaling that cinnamon and clove scent felt intoxicating, and there was no end in sight to this snow-in.

Yet against all my better judgment, I let out a breath and said, "Okay."

<h1 style="text-align:center">Thirteen</h1>

Elowyn

Liam and I stood side by side as he rattled off ingredients, and I laid them all out on the wooden island in front of us.

"Eggs," he said.

"Check."

"Flour."

"Check."

"Sugar—hey!" he yelled.

I batted down the piece of parchment in his hands, and it floated to the table. "Can we just get on with the baking part?"

I bounced on my heels, getting that itch I always got where I just wanted to start. Enough with the planning and checking and double checking. I appreciated Liam's thoroughness, but at some point, we needed to actually cook.

He shoved a hand through his blonde waves, a few strands falling over his forehead that I had the urge to brush away. I curled my hand into a tight fist, annoyed with the pervasive thoughts that had started after that night we slept next to each other.

"I think we can start." I slid the parchment away as he tried to grab it. "If we forget an ingredient, we can just grab it out of the pantry."

He crossed his muscled arms over his chest, the definition stark under his tunic. I hated that I was even noticing these things. Thankfully, I'd had no more dreams about him, but now that I'd had one, I couldn't stop thinking about it. Thinking about how it would actually feel to unravel this so perfectly put-together man. To see what stoic, reserved Liam was like when he fully let go.

"Are you going to start?" he asked, brow arched.

I cleared my throat, willing the heat prickling over the most sensitive parts of my body to turn to ice.

I reached for the sifter, but paused as one of the measuring cups floated up in front of me. I reached out to touch it, but Liam grabbed my arm.

"Just wait and watch," he said with a smirk.

The measuring cup dipped into the bag of flour, reemerging with a perfectly level cupful. The sifter floated over the bowl, and the measuring cup dumped the flour into it as the little crank on the sifter began turning. Flour strained through its holes into the mixing bowl, my mouth agape the entire time.

"What is happening right now?"

Liam smiled. "Magic."

"The kitchen can actually do all this?"

I turned back as the measuring cup added more flour to the sifter.

"I told you magic was unpredictable. The kitchen helps when it wants to. Castle decides."

"You just said Castle like it's a name," I said. "Like the castle has a name that you use to address it."

He leaned forward, voice dropping into a whisper that brushed against my skin, goosebumps prickling over my arms. "It does. But you don't get to use its name until Castle gets used to you. Use it too early, act like you're too familiar with Castle, and it'll make you pay."

I didn't ask for details, not wanting to know all the ways this castle could punish people.

Pops and swirls of blue magic trailed after the moving kitchen utensils. "This is amazing."

I'd seen magic plenty. It was impossible to avoid it in our world, where it was threaded so deeply into everything. But I'd never seen a magical kitchen. I'd never had magic aid me in anything, and it felt a little bit like working side by side with the ancient godwitch of food and wine, like maybe, they were telling us that we were on the right path, that working together was pleasing them.

"I guess we do make a good team," Liam said, like he was thinking the same thing that I was. "Now." His gaze dipped to the parchment on the counter. "What's next on the recipe?"

Two hours later, we admired a three tier cake, iced with white frosting. I'd impulsively added pomegranate seeds on top as decoration.

"Wow." Liam slung a dish rag over his shoulder, flour smudged across his cheek. "This looks amazing." He turned. "I was thinking . . ." He trailed off, plucking a few sprigs of mint leaves from a bowl and carefully placing them next to the pomegranate seeds, adding beautiful pops of green that added festivity to the cake, perfect for the Winter Solstice theme.

"Hold on." I pointed to the parchment laying forgotten on the counter. "Did you just add something that wasn't on the recipe?"

He rolled his eyes. "I thought it might be a nice complement to the pomegranate."

"But you just spontaneously added it."

His lips tipped up at the corner. "Uh-huh."

"Am I influencing you?" I asked. "I'm flattered."

"Don't get too excited. It's just some mint. It might taste terrible with the pomegranate."

"But it might not." I waggled my eyebrows, and he laughed.

"Just cut the cake," he said.

We turned to a much smaller cake sitting next to the bigger one to try. I held up a fork. "Do you want to do the honors?"

Liam pushed the fork toward me. "No, this is your creation. Your genius."

"It's ours," I argued.

"You're the one who thought of adding white wine and pomegranate juice. This was just supposed to be a simple vanilla cake."

"And you're the one who kept me on track and talked me out of adding pomegranate seeds directly into the cake. Somebody either would've choked or cracked a tooth."

He grabbed a fork. "Okay, then how about we both try it at the same time?"

We clinked forks, then dug in, and I shoved a bite of the red cake into my mouth.

Oh. Oh, godwitches.

Liam chewed, his face not betraying any emotion while I let out a moan, the tartness of the white wine a perfect compliment to the sweetness of the pomegranate juice—and the thin layer of sugary frosting balanced it all out with a refreshing pop of mint at the end.

"Holy fuck," Liam said through a mouthful. "That's good."

I finished swallowing my bite. "Finally!"

"What?" he asked.

"I had no idea what you were thinking. You might as well have been eating sprouts for all I knew."

"Hey, no need to insult sprouts."

"They're disgusting."

"That's because you haven't tried mine."

I stuck my fork in for another bite. "That cake is going to be a hit."

"It's the perfect Winter Solstice dessert."

"We did it," I said. "We made something divine." I squealed and without thinking threw my arms around Liam's neck.

He caught me, his hands coming to my waist, pinning me to his hard body, and suddenly, I was having flashbacks to that night we cuddled together under his blanket.

The smile faded from my lips as we locked gazes.

He licked his lips. "You have something." He set me down, keeping one hand on my waist while the other brushed frosting from my lip, his fingers rough against my skin.

His thumb came away, the white frosting still on it, and he brought it to his mouth and sucked it off.

I inhaled sharply, staring at his lips, wondering if they'd taste as good in real life as they had in my dream.

Liam leaned down, ever so slightly, almost imperceptibly. If I just tipped up my chin, our lips could brush, and I could finally see if he was all that my dreams made him out to be.

"Oh, look, Barty," a voice said. "They're over here in front of their warm fire, eating cake, not even caring about the fact that we've been buried in the snow."

Both of us whipped around at the same time to see two angry gargoyle faces staring at us from the windows on either side of the door.

"You know, I'm really starting to feel under appreciated," Tal said.

Liam quickly removed his hand from my waist, and I felt the painful, cold absence of it immediately. "Barty?" He rushed forward, opening the door.

To my shock, a winding pathway had been carved out of the snow, leading out into the garden. "Tal!"

He threw an arm around the gargoyle on the right, who recoiled. "Oh, sure. It's all hugs now, but where were you when we were drowning in snow?"

"You're statues," Liam said. "You can't drown. You know that, right?"

"That is so insensitive." Barty crossed his arms. "You're welcome by the way. Our heads finally got free, and we blew the snow away to for you."

"You can do that?" I asked, temporarily distracted.

"Gargoyle magic." Tal sniffed. "Very powerful breath."

I watched the exchange while my brain tried to catch up to what was happening. The snow was cleared. We weren't trapped anymore. I could leave. I didn't understand why that thought was so devastating. We couldn't have stayed trapped in this little kitchen forever, just the two of us. It was ludicrous to even want that.

But some small part of me did want it. It was a horrifying, exhilarating, terrifying revelation.

Liam turned, smile so luminous it was clear he harbored none of the complicated feelings currently coursing through me.

Tears unexpectedly sprang to my eyes, so ridiculous and so out of character, I did the only thing I could think of. I shoved past him and ran right out the door.

Fourteen

LIAM

"Where is she going?" Barty pointed at Elowyn, who ran through the snow, mahogany hair blowing in the wind. Her figure dipped in out of view as she wove through the path carved out in the snow.

I didn't even think as I took off after her.

"Hey!" Barty called. "A 'thank you' would be nice!"

Something had upset her, and I had no idea what. I thought she'd be happy, relieved, that we weren't trapped anymore, but when I'd turned to smile at her, it had looked like she'd been punched in the gut.

I had to go after her and find out what had upset her so greatly.

Right before Barty had spoken, I'd made the first move. I'd shifted, and I could've sworn something like desire flashed in her eyes.

Now I had to know if that almost kiss between us haunted her as much as it was already haunting me. Nothing could come of this, not with how much our families hated each other, yet my legs kept moving, my arms pumping until I was just one stride away from her. I grabbed her arm, and she whirled to face me, chest heaving, eyes rimmed with red. Frosted breath puffed from her mouth, walls of snow surrounding us, making it feel like we were in our own private winter wonderland.

"You're crying."

She sniffled. "Just upset I didn't have a chance to stab you and make my nan proud."

I laughed and thumbed away a tear trailing down her cheek. "Uh-huh. I've seen you with a knife, you know. You almost chopped off your own thumb slicing carrots."

She laughed, too, and soon we were both laughing, our breaths crystallizing into clouds, mixing between us.

"Why were you crying, Elowyn?" I put both hands on her arms, gently rubbing them up and down.

She licked her lips, searching my face, and something in my expression must've made her walls crumble. "Because I'm going to miss you," she said. "Because the last three days we've been in this little alternate world where you and I could be friends." The word stung, but then she said, "Where we could be more than friends."

"Elowyn." I stepped closer, this time, moving my hands to her back and sweeping her into my arms.

She sucked in a sharp breath but didn't push me away, head tipping back so she could gaze up at me. "This is impossible, Liam. You know that. You know why."

"All I know is that if I don't kiss you right this second I'm going to regret it for the rest of my life. It will eat at me every damn day." I leaned down, my lips lingering right over hers, the invitation there for the taking, but she'd have to meet me, she'd have to make the final decision.

I hovered there, my mouth so fucking close to capturing hers, for what felt like an eternity. So long that I was sure at any moment she'd shove me away and tell me I'd lost my mind.

Then the impossible happened. She rose up on her tiptoes and pressed her mouth to mine. Every bit of cold melted in my body. The kiss started out hesitant in a way that surprised me from Elowyn, who was usually so take charge and decisive.

I let out a growl and kissed her hard, kissed her like it might be the only chance I ever got. She tasted as good as she smelled, hints of cinnamon lingering on her tongue from all the baking we'd done this morning, and suddenly, I was fucking ravenous.

"Godwitches, you taste divine," I said between kisses.

She gripped my shirt in her fists, tugging me closer as if she couldn't get enough of me either. I urged her mouth open with mine and swiped my tongue along hers. She moaned into my lips, her grip on my shirt getting tighter as I devoured her with my mouth, our kisses growing hungrier, my body growing hungrier. All for her.

I was kissing Elowyn Carragh. I was kissing Elowyn—and I liked it. I didn't want to stop, and I was afraid that if I did, that would be it, that I'd never get a taste of her again. The thought only made me kiss her harder, made my mouth more frenzied with need as it moved against hers over and over.

"Liam!" Father called from somewhere in this never-ending maze the gargoyles had carved into the snow.

"Elowyn?" came Ms. Carragh's worried voice.

It was like a cleaver struck us apart, and we both jumped back, breathing heavy, the air clouding in front of us.

We stared at each other, Elowyn's fingers coming to her reddened, plump lips, eyes wide in horror.

"Elowyn! What in the godwitches are you doing without your cloak in this weather?" Her nan appeared from around a corner of the pathway and ran toward Elowyn, wrapping her frail arms around her granddaughter while Elowyn continued staring at me in shock.

"Son, what's going on out here?" My father appeared, cheeks red from the cold, and he rubbed his gloved hands together.

Elowyn's nan jabbed a finger in my direction. "Did you lead her out here to give her pneumonia? Well, joke's on you because we Carraghs don't get sick. Not with my special broth I make whenever anyone has a cold coming on."

"No." Elowyn shook her head. "I . . . ran away."

Ms. Carragh's eyes snapped to her. "What are you talking about? Why would you run away from your job?"

Elowyn's mouth opened and closed, and I could tell she didn't know what to say.

I stepped forward. "She saw the gargoyles had parted the snow and was excited to get out of the kitchen after three days stuck inside."

"Y-yes, exactly," Elowyn said.

My father's gaze bounced between the two of us, but he didn't speak, just observed with that discerning gaze that always made me feel like he saw right through me. "Your sister has been worried, you know," he said.

"Ava?" I asked, doubtful that was true. Ava was a typical teenager and didn't care about anyone but herself.

"Yes, Ava," Father said, irritation lacing his voice. "She's been acting odd, talking about how she was afraid she'd never see you again."

That made no sense. I wasn't dead. Just snowed in.

Elowyn's eyes widened, and she shot me a look of horror I didn't understand. "You should go to your sister," she said. "Talk to her. Listen to her." She emphasized each word like it had a secret meaning, but I wasn't following.

"Let me get my cloak, and we'll go home," Elowyn said to her grandmother.

"What about the feast?" I almost reached for her but curled my hand into a fist to stop myself. "We still have a lot to do."

Elowyn didn't meet my gaze.

"You've been working three days straight!" Her nan shook a finger at me. "An afternoon off won't kill either of you, and my poor girl needs a warm bath and some food." Her eyebrows drew into a scowl. "Have you been eating?"

Elowyn let out a soft breath, and it reminded me of the way her warm breath had grazed my skin right before I'd kissed her.

"I'll see you in the morning, then," I said, the thought of being away from her for an entire night unbearable.

How had I gone from not wanting to spend a second with Elowyn to wanting to spend every second with her?

Her nan put an arm around her as they started walking back toward the kitchen to collect her cloak, speaking in hushed tones.

I wanted—needed—more of Elowyn. I'd gotten a taste of her, and now I was hooked, but as I watched her walk away without so much as a backward glance, I wondered if she felt the same. A sinking feeling in my gut told me that I already knew the answer, and I wouldn't like it.

Fifteen

ELOWYN

Nan sniffed the air as if she could smell the secret I was hiding.

We walked through a winter wonderland, Fairwitch carpeted in glittering white snow, pristine under the glowing sun, which felt so good on my face.

"What are you doing?" I asked, putting distance between us.

Today, I was actually wearing appropriate clothing for the weather: blue stockings, brown boots, and a thick wool dress, layered with a blue scarf and a cloak. I breathed in the clean, crisp scent.

Townspeople littered the street, shoveling snow into tall piles to make pathways.

"You're acting odd," Nan said, eyeing me. "You've been acting odd ever since I found you and Liam in that garden yesterday. What was he doing out there with you? You never did tell me."

What was he doing out there with me? Defiling me with his mouth in the absolute best way. Filling me with a need so fierce it terrified me. Kissing me like no man had ever kissed me before, like I suspected no man would ever kiss me again.

"Nothing," I said, gloved hands twisting together in front of me.

"He followed me out there. Both of us were so excited to finally be free of our prison, we ran out here without thinking."

Nan eyed me suspiciously. She'd insisted on walking me to the castle this morning, even though I'd said it wasn't necessary. Mama and Papa had told me to stop arguing and let Nan do what she wanted.

"Hm," she said.

We entered the castle gardens through an archway and passed under trees that looked like they'd been carved from ice. Crystal-like icicles hung from the branches, the sun punching through them and splashing a rainbow of colors onto the snow.

If I wasn't so wrecked by what had happened between me and Liam, I might actually be able to take all of this beauty in, to appreciate it.

"So how has it been? Cooking with that boy?"

I snorted. At thirty, Liam was not a boy, and he most definitely did not kiss like one. No, the way he'd kissed me had been all man. I doused the desire burning in my belly at the memory of his lips, so soft and warm and perfect.

"I already told you," I said. "When you were at the dumbwaiter every day, barking down questions."

Nan rolled her eyes. "Not the answer you gave me in front of him. The real answer. Now that he's not around and you can be honest."

"It's fine. Honestly. We have a job to get done, and we're on the same team. Team Don't Ruin Winter Solstice Feast. That makes it a bit easier to work together."

"What's his weakness?" Nan asked. "There's a reason Prince Cillian invited you to cook for him, you know. Liam isn't cutting it, and I think the prince might be in the market for a new chef."

The thought didn't fill me with as much glee as it should have. Yes, I badly wanted that job, but not when it would come at Liam's expense.

"What is the matter with you?" Nan shook a finger. "Blink twice if you're being controlled."

I rolled my eyes. "Nan, I'm trying to be professional. I want to do my best, and I can't do that if I'm fighting with Liam." I debated saying my next words but couldn't help myself. "Why do we have to fight with the Wolverns anyway? Once upon a time, the Carraghs and Wolverns worked together. One restaurant and bakery that shared a space and patrons."

Nan lifted her sharp, pointy chin. "That was before they stooped to cheating."

"We don't even have proof of it," I said. "It was centuries ago. Can't we just move on from the whole thing?"

Nan stopped abruptly, and I realized what a horrible mistake I'd just made.

"Stop the whole thing? Stop hating the family that has plagued us for years, tried to take our birthright from us? The family that has cheated and lied and stolen from us?" Her gaze softened, and she put a hand on my shoulder. "Elowyn, I understand. There was a time when I had the same thoughts."

We continued walking, a wind blowing errant snowflakes past us.

"There was a time I'd wanted to be friends with Liam's grandmother. She had it all. Beauty, intelligence, grit. I admired her and thought maybe if we formed a friendship, we could end the rivalry between our families."

"What happened?" I asked, knowing I didn't want to hear the answer, but it was coming either way.

Nan wove her arm through mine, clutching to me tightly. "We did become friends, and it almost ran the Deerborn into the ground."

"Why?" I asked. I should've been horrified at the thought of our family business not even existing by the time I was born—but instead, it felt like a missed opportunity. If there was no business, would I have the freedom to cook how I wanted? To lean into my true self?

I shook my head as Nan continued.

"Our families didn't approve of the friendship, naturally. But it made their fighting worse. Made the rivalry between us rise to new heights neither of us could've predicted. That was when she betrayed me. Her family got to her, in the end, convinced her she could be of service to them, would make them proud if she sabotaged us. So that's what she did. She used one of the lorealos flowers that grow up in the hills during springtime. Ground them up into dust and added that dust to all our food."

I gasped. The lorealos flower came from the earth godwitch's magic and was poisonous when ingested. It was great for salves, healing cuts and burns and rashes—but when eaten, it could cause horrible stomach issues.

"Half the town got sick from our food, and our reputation suffered for it."

My mind raced at this information. "How do you know it was her?"

"She admitted it." Nan's chin wobbled, and that small show of emotion surprised me. That betrayal still affected Nan to this day. "Felt so bad she confessed. I ended our friendship right then and there and realized I could never trust a Wolvern, ever again. And neither can you. That boy is loyal to his family above all else."

I thought of what Liam had revealed to me, how he worked that job because it was what his father wanted for him. He did it so he could live out his dad's dreams.

A pit formed in my stomach at Nan's words, and I couldn't bring myself to argue, to cause any more distress than I already had. This rivalry was woven into our blood, and nothing I could say would change that, but more than that . . . if I allowed myself to fall for Liam, and he betrayed me, it would break my heart. "You're right, Nan." I gestured toward the kitchen, wondering if Liam was already in there, getting ready for the day. "We're here."

I pressed a quick kiss to Nan's cheek.

"Knock 'em dead," she said, turning and walking away.

I waved goodbye. "I always do."

I turned toward the kitchen, not knowing how I was going to walk inside and cook next to Liam and pretend like nothing had changed between us. But that was exactly what I had to do. My family would never approve, and how was I supposed to take the job of a man I was falling for? I couldn't. So the answer was simple: I'd shove these feelings down and act like that kiss never happened. I'd go back to hating Liam Wolvern so I could do what I needed to get the royal chef job.

I raised my head high and walked into the kitchen.

WHAT I DIDN'T COUNT on was walking into the kitchen to see Liam standing there, sunlight pouring in and haloing him like some other-worldly being.

The front laces on his light blue tunic showed his muscled chest, covered in thick blonde curls. His arms flexed as he minced garlic, his sleeves rolled up to reveal muscular forearms.

Godwitches be. Forearms. His forearms were sending flutters through my belly. He shook the blonde cowlicks out of his eyes, his wavy hair shimmering.

He looked up, brown eyes twinkling. "Are you just going to stand there? You're letting cold air in." He pointed his knife toward the open door behind me, which I'd completely forgotten about.

"Uh, yes. No, I mean." I turned and closed the door, taking a few deep breaths to ground myself before I walked up the stairs to face him. "Good morning," I said, keeping my voice as airy as possible.

I joined him at the counter, peering at the list of things we'd need to get done today. The feast was in just two days, but thanks to our teamwork, we were actually on schedule.

Today we needed to marinate all the meat and get it ready to be cooked tomorrow, where most of it would slow cook until the feast.

We had leg of lamb, stuffed chickens, and a boar that would roast over the hearth on a spit.

"Hey," Liam said. "Can we talk about yesterday?"

I squeezed my eyes shut. Talking about our kiss would be the adult thing to do, but I was already wilting under the heat of his gaze on me, avoiding eye contact at all costs. "I think it's better we don't."

He stilled, his knife no longer moving. "Really?" A mixture of surprise and hurt filled his voice, and my heart fractured. I didn't want to hurt him, but if I took anything away from Nan's story, it was that this was for the best.

Pretending nothing had happened over the last three days would save us both from a world of pain in the future. We would hurt each other eventually. It was inevitable, no matter how much we didn't want to believe it.

"It was a kiss, fueled by our excitement over getting out of this kitchen." I still didn't meet his gaze. "Look, Liam, we both know that as soon as we're done working together, things will go back exactly the way they were. And that's how it should be. So let's just focus on why we're here. We can't afford any distractions."

Silence followed, and sweat beaded my forehead as I waited for his response.

"Right" was all he said, and I breathed out a sigh of relief as that rhythmic thwack of the knife filled the room.

I looked down at the list and moved toward the pantry to grab the ingredients for the stuffing when Liam grabbed my arm and spun me to face him.

He was doing that a lot these days, and every damn time it made my heart skip a beat.

"No," he said firmly.

"No, what?" I asked as his heated gaze raked over me, my knees going weak.

"No we're not going to pretend that kiss didn't happen." He walked me backward until my back was pressed against the brick wall. "There is no going back after that," he said, voice deep and low, pinpricks of desire rippling across me. "I don't care about our family rivalry. I don't care that we've spent the majority of our lives hating each other. I don't care that my father will likely disown me for admitting my feelings for you."

That took me aback. "F-feelings?" I asked. There was clearly something between us, but I'd thought it was physical, not anything beyond that. "What if we hurt each other?" I asked. "What if . . . what if I get this chef job and you lose it? What happens then?"

He paused. I expected him to tell me that I was right, that that could very well happen and maybe he hadn't thought things through.

But instead, he said, "So what if that does happen?"

A disbelieving laugh escaped me, his arms still caging me, his body still pinning me, making me want to pounce on him. "You'll hate me and resent me. We wouldn't survive something like that."

"I think we could," Liam said, rubbing his jaw before placing his hand back against the wall. "Elowyn, I talked to my sister last night. Just like you told me to."

I shook my head, wondering if maybe Liam had inhaled too much smoke this morning. "What does that mean?"

"You knew. You knew she was planning something."

I bit my lip. "I overheard her a day before I came to work with you in the kitchen. I didn't hear everything, but it sounded like she was planning something."

Liam nodded. "Planning to run away from home. And it was because of me. She's the only one who saw through my facade and has known how unhappy I've been in this role. She thought if she ran away, then the pressure would be gone, that I could quit and not worry about my father moving onto her as his one big hope. She wanted to protect me. To free me. It made me realize what a coward I've been. This whole time I thought I was the one protecting her. That by doing my father's bidding and living out his dream, I could save Ava from that future, from that chokehold, but all I was doing was showing her how to be unhappy and not go after what you want in life."

"You don't want to be a chef? But you love cooking." I couldn't believe what I was hearing.

"I do, but I don't love this job. I hate being in charge of everything all the time. I hate the pressure. I hate the lack of routine. I hate the decision-making. I'm not meant to run a kitchen. I just want to cook in one. But you, Elowyn, you would thrive in an environment like this. It would give you the excitement you crave." He cupped my cheek. "That you deserve so you can be yourself and stop dimming your creativity and genius to cater to your family."

My eyes welled with tears at his admission, at the fact that he knew exactly what I needed to thrive, that instead of looking down on my impulsiveness, he saw it as a strength. "It'll still cause problems between our families, even if we're happy with these choices." I couldn't keep the tremble out of my voice.

He nodded. "It could, but I don't give a fuck. Ava deserves a good role model. She deserves to see a healthy example of being true to yourself."

My eyes widened as he leaned in, breath hot on my skin.

"Ava wanting to run away was a wake-up call, one that reminded me we have a single life to live, and I'm done living for someone else. I'm done living to please my father and fulfill his dreams while letting mine slip away. I want to cook, but I also want to have a life."

Everything he was saying made so much sense. Even though Liam and I were different, we'd been doing the same thing, placating our families at our own expense.

I trailed a finger down his chest. I'd wanted to touch him ever since I walked into this kitchen today. "What else do you want?"

His lips quirked, and then his hands dropped to my ass as he lifted me. On instinct, my legs wrapped around his waist as he walked me toward the counter, setting me on top of it. "I think it's better if I show you the answer to that question."

Sixteen

His lips crashed into mine, and all thoughts of our families, of the upcoming feast, fled. I placed my hands on his broad shoulders, the muscles contracting under my palms. Just like the other day, this kiss sent my body reeling.

His cock strained against his trousers, and I felt every bit of his long length as I pressed my pelvis into him, making him groan.

He might've not wanted to run a kitchen, but he absolutely knew how to command my body, make me melt right into him, and all he'd done so far was kiss me. I couldn't imagine what would happen when he got me naked, when his lips roamed to other places.

We kissed like that for a long time, savoring and enjoying the taste of each other. His fingers came down to my ass and trailed up and down my back, sending fresh waves of heat through me every time he touched a new spot.

"How do you do this to me?" he asked in that raspy voice he only used when he was turned on, a sound I was very close to becoming addicted to.

"Maybe it's the potion I used?" I asked with a teasing tone. "Figured making the competition obsessed with me would be a good distraction."

He gently lay me on my back, and I gasped at the quick change in position, at the hard counter under me. "There's just one problem with your plan," he said.

"What's that?" I asked.

"You're obsessed with me too." He lifted my dress, pressing kisses against my inner thighs, and a shudder ran through me as I half-laughed, half-moaned.

"I guess I should let the alchemists handle potions and I should stick to cooking." I gasped as he slid my panties down my legs until they stretched between my ankles.

He parted my folds. "So wet," he murmured. "Is that all for me?"

At this point, words weren't forming, so I managed a "mm-hmm" as he swiped a finger down my center. He stood tall and put his finger in his mouth, sucking and moaning.

"De-fucking-licious."

Godwitches be. This man could not be real. It should've been so jarring that Liam Wolvern, a person I'd hated my entire life, was kissing me and filling me with a desire I hadn't felt in a long time. This should've felt wrong, but it didn't. It was the opposite. Like this was what we should've been doing all along.

He dipped his head back down, licking up my center, and I arched my pelvis upward as he rubbed his face against me, the rasp of his stubble igniting my body.

I half sat up, propped on my elbows, wanting this, but wanting him more. I wanted to know what it would be like to have Liam inside of me, and I'd never been one for patience. We didn't have all day to lay around in bed. This might be the only chance I got to enjoy his body, and damnit, I wanted to.

"Liam." I gasped as he licked again. "I need you. I need to feel you inside of me."

He straightened again, pupils blown, and he licked his lips. "I like the way that sounds."

I fully sat up, grabbing the laces of his trousers, and undoing them. He pulled his waistband down, and his cock sprang free, a bead of moisture on the tip. He was long and hard and I already knew that after this there would be no going back. After I experienced Liam inside of me, I'd crave him like I craved no other man. He grabbed my hips and tugged me forward until I was on the edge of the counter, and he was slipping inside of me with the same need I felt.

We both gasped when he slid all the way in, and I threw my arms around his neck, clinging to him as he pumped in and out.

"I knew it," I said, rocking my hips and riding his length.

"Knew what?" he asked into my shoulder, gently nipping at it.

"That you'd ruin me. That there would be no going back after you."

"You've already ruined me," he said, drawing out of me, and I instantly craved him, craved filling the emptiness he'd left. He looked at me, such tenderness in his gaze. "The moment you walked in this kitchen, I think part of me knew I was yours. Or, at least, that I wanted to be."

"When did you become so good with words?" I reached for him, drawing his face to mine and kissing him fiercely.

"I guess you bring it out in me," he said, then slammed back into me, liquefying my insides.

We kissed while he ravaged me, and I wiggled against him, loving the friction of his long length rough against my clit every time he pulled out.

A moan escaped me, and he let me take over the pace as I rode him and rolled my hips, faster, faster until I was nothing but molten, reaching a breaking point, edging closer to tipping into oblivion.

"Godwitches, you're so tight," he said.

I threw my head back, spots dotting my vision as I came apart. My walls clenched around him, wringing every single drop of his own orgasm from him.

One last pulse of pleasure rolled through me before I slumped into Liam, holding tight, his heart hammering against my ear. My thighs quivered, my body completely spent.

He rested his head on top of mine and let out a soft laugh. "Why haven't we been doing this all along?"

I drew back to look at his mussed hair, swollen lips, and the sheen of sweat on his skin. "I guess we were too busy fighting."

He kissed me. "But this is so much better."

"If only we knew," I said.

"Well, now we do, and I'm never going back, Elowyn Carragh."

I wasn't either, and that was what terrified me the most.

Seventeen

LIAM

Holy shit. I wanted to kick myself for wasting so much time fighting Elowyn all these years when I could've been fucking her instead.

I was still inside of her, my cock slick from her orgasm, from my orgasm, and I didn't want to pull out, didn't want to get to work, even though we had to. We might've been on schedule, but that didn't mean we could afford to waste any time.

Not that I'd ever count having sex with Elowyn as a waste of time. I might actually be willing to let this entire winter feast go up in flames if it meant doing that again.

"We need to get to work," she murmured, but she didn't show any inclination to move, her head resting on my chest as I inhaled cinnamon and clove.

"I think you might be my new favorite flavor," I said, and she laughed.

I wasn't sure I'd ever get used to being the cause of that sound. I'd never known how intoxicating it would be to be the one how made her do it.

She wiggled her hips while I was still lodged firmly inside of her, and my cock twitched.

"You're going to be the death of me," I said.

"That would be a shame since we just started getting along so well."

"Liam!" My father's voice rang out over the castle gardens.

In an instant, the atmosphere went from lazy and satisfied to tense. Elowyn shrieked and jolted, hopping off the counter and dropping to her knees, looking for her panties. I yanked up my trousers, lacing them as quickly as humanly possible.

"Here." I kicked her silky white panties toward her, and she grappled with them, pulling them on and hopping up as my father approached.

"What is he doing here?" Elowyn frantically combed her fingers through her strands. "Does my hair look like nothing happened?" She pointed at her tousled mahogany hair, mussed and showing signs of my hands bunching it over and over.

"Yes," I lied. "You look great."

She nodded, spinning to face the door right as it burst open, my father stepping into the space, followed by Elowyn's nan.

Her nan elbowed my father out of the way.

"Nan, you're supposed to be back at the Deerborn," Elowyn said, tucking her hair behind her ear.

Ms. Carragh hooked her thumb toward my father. "Saw him creeping out of their bakery, and I decided to follow. I knew he was coming to cause trouble."

I crossed my arms as Elowyn groaned. "I thought we talked about this. We need to be able to work together to pull this feast off. We can't do that if you two are constantly lurking."

My father held up his hands. "No one is fighting. I just came to check in and make sure everything is on track since Liam has been so tight-lipped about what you two have been getting up to in this kitchen."

Elowyn choked, coughing as I hid a smile behind my fist.

My father shot her an annoyed look, and I had the urge to punch him.

"We've been cooking," I said as Elowyn cleared her throat, cheeks adorably flushed pink. "That's generally what you do in a kitchen, Father."

Elowyn made an imperceptible sound, and her nan's sharp gaze landed on her.

"And we have a lot of cooking to do as Elowyn already mentioned." I stalked toward them, hands out, ushering them both toward the door.

"We just got here," Elowyn's nan said.

"And now you're going to have to leave. This is my kitchen, and I'm putting my foot down. You two can't just barge in. We're not snowed in anymore, and you don't have an excuse to be here. Go home. Let us work."

Elowyn's nan and my father shot each other uneasy looks, but as I swung the door open, neither argued, both of them leaving.

I shut the door and pressed my back against it, relief sweeping over me that they were finally gone.

Elowyn pressed her lips together, then burst out laughing.

Every time she laughed, it lit up the space she was in, and this was no different. I couldn't help the smile that came to my face.

"I can't believe we just had sex on the kitchen counter." She pointed right where I'd had her pinned just moments ago. Her gaze turned sultry as she walked toward me, hips sashaying. "I have to admit, Eamon, that was very sexy how you just took charge." She stopped in front of me, tipping her chin up, gaze heated in a way that stirred my blood.

"Elowyn," I said, lips nearly touching hers. "Please don't ever call me Eamon again."

It reminded me far too much of my father, and honestly? I had zero desire to be thinking about him right now.

"Should we start cooking?" she asked, our mouths still impossibly close but somehow not touching.

"We should," I said, my willpower ebbing away with each second I felt her warm breath on my lips. I grabbed her hips and tugged her into me. "But I think maybe we deserve a little break after all our hard work."

"We definitely do," she agreed.

Our mouths collided, my hand dipping down under her skirt and rubbing against her damp panties while she moaned into my mouth.

"Later," I said, rubbing quicker, frenzied circles as she arched into me. "We'll get to work later."

Eighteen

ELOWYN

My head rested on Liam's chest, both of us lying on his bed pallet in front of a roaring fire. It was early afternoon, and we still hadn't gotten to work, yet I felt more at peace, more myself, than I had in years. I felt like I was finally waking up and realizing I didn't have to follow in my family's path to keep the family peace. Not when it came at the expense of my own peace.

Liam didn't want this chef job, but that didn't mean I would get it. The final decision was up to Prince Cillian, and if he didn't choose me, then I would be okay. I could take my creativity in the kitchen anywhere. I didn't have to stay stuck in the past if my family chose to. I loved them, and I always would, but I was done being held back by them.

"What's going on in that mind of yours?" Liam murmured into my hair.

"Just thinking about the future."

He tensed, and I wondered what about those words caused him stress. Maybe he was thinking about his future, how he was going to have to tell his father he wanted to follow his own dreams.

"What's going to happen with us outside of this kitchen?" he asked, and it was my turn to tense.

In here it felt like our own secret little world where no one else could ruin what we had. But in the real world, we'd have to deal with our families, with society, with all the stress that came with living in a magical town that was hidden from the rest of the world to keep it safe.

"I don't know," I said honestly. I propped myself on an elbow to look at him, the fire washing him in its warm glow. "I like you, and I like what we've been doing in the kitchen." I leaned down to kiss him. "I don't think I'm ready to tell our families, though."

His brows creased.

"We don't even know what this is yet. We haven't talked about it." I was rambling, but somehow, I couldn't stop. "Are we ready for a relationship? Especially when both of us are about to break our families' hearts. You're going to tell your father you don't want to be the royal chef anymore. I'm going to tell my family I don't want to work at Deerborn anymore. That's already a lot for them to take."

His finger twisted in a strand of my hair. "Let's take it slow, then. Let's do more of this." He leaned up and kissed me, slow and languid, his tongue rolling over my lips and pushing into my mouth, making my knees go weak. "It'll be our secret."

Relief washed over me that this didn't have to end. Not yet.

Liam sat up, swiping a hand through his hair. "We do, actually, have to get to work now."

I groaned, knowing he was right. Back to reality sooner than I'd wanted.

"I'm going to miss being in the kitchen with you." I stood and pulled my dress over my head while Liam tugged his trousers on.

"Really?" He arched a brow. "Are you telling me you're starting to like all my lists?"

I let out a laugh as I grabbed my apron and tied it around my back. "It keeps me on task and from implementing so many new ideas that I ruin the entire thing. Your lists and schedules rein me in while still allowing me to indulge in my favorite parts of cooking."

He stared at me for a beat, his expression unreadable, and I wondered what was going on in that brain of his.

"Yeah," he said. "You know, I haven't felt that normal anxiety I get in the kitchen with you around. I know if something goes wrong or unexpectedly pops up, you'll be by my side to help handle it."

I stood in front of the plucked chicken, which still needed to be stuffed with a creamy thick herbed cheese that I'd made. "I guess we actually do make a great team. A Wolvern and a Carragh. Who would've thought?"

Before I could grab the bowl of cheese, the cloth lifted from it, and then the bowl spun up into the air, wisps of blue shimmers surrounding it.

I stepped back, staring in awe.

The bowl tipped upside down, and the cheese mixture fell out and swooped right into the opening I'd cut in the chicken's stomach, where I'd pulled out all the entrails and organs to serve in various side dishes.

Liam scratched his head as a knife whizzed past him, followed by garlic, onion, and carrots that all dropped onto a cutting board as the knife began chopping furiously. "I don't know." He looked on in wonder as the kitchen came alive around us.

I'd seen bits and pieces of the castle's magic, but nothing like this where everything was suddenly just . . . functioning.

The clay oven sparked to life, flames jumping and popping, and a covered bowl with the rising dough I'd made yesterday dumped out onto a wooden baking sheet, which then slid right into the oven.

Liam and I sent each other confused looks as icy blue and white magic shimmered in the air while pots, pans, and knives flew in various directions.

"What is going on?" I asked.

Liam scratched his head. "I've never seen the kitchen do this before."

"Maybe it knows we need help?" I suggested, ducking as a bowl flew toward my head.

"But we needed help the night we didn't have a fire," Liam said. "I mean, we were shivering, on the brink of hypothermia, and had no choice but to sleep together . . ."

That had been the night I'd that sex dream about Liam, the night my feelings started shifting and I was seeing him in a different light.

I gasped. "Maybe the kitchen needs harmony and peace in order for the magic to work. Or maybe it just wants that."

A whisk plopped into a bowl nearby, the marinade for the boar already almost done and mixed.

"Well, it's nice to know us kissing makes someone happy."

Liam let out a soft laugh and came up behind me, wrapping his arms around my waist and nuzzling my neck. "Does that mean we can do more kissing? It looks like the kitchen has a pretty good handle on the feast."

He nipped my earlobe, and my toes curled as I turned into him while he dragged his lips down my jawline until I wasn't thinking about the winter feast anymore. And then when his hand dipped under my dress, thumb rubbing my peaked nipple, I wasn't thinking about anything at all.

Nineteen

LIAM

Garlands of green stretched between the tall white bannisters of the great hall. Sprigs of holly decorated the long rectangular tables, where the people of Fairwitch sat and ate and chattered. Things had been hard in Fairwitch lately with the mysterious attacks and uncertainty about the future, but today everyone could be grateful and celebrate what we did have.

This might've been my favorite part of cooking, creating food that brought everyone together. I locked eyes with Elowyn across the room, where she sat with her nan, mother, and father. She wore a gorgeous velvet green dress that molded to her body, the long sleeves hanging off her shoulders and exposing her collarbone that I'd dragged my mouth across earlier this morning.

My father clinked his crystal glass against mine, and I turned to him, taking a sip of the sparkling wine. "Well done, son." He nodded to the huge boar that sat on a raised table in front of the high prince's throne. "I'm impressed you pulled this off. Some of the recipes are a little unconventional." He wrinkled his nose at the sesame and poppyseed loaf that Elowyn had made.

"Yet people love it," I argued, anger flaring in my chest at his dig toward Elowyn. "And new isn't always bad."

"No, I suppose not, but all I care about is that you're staying in that kitchen." He took a sip of his wine. "And it looks like you will be. The Carraghs might've had other ideas, but you, my boy, you didn't let me down."

That familiar tightness spread across my chest like it did every time my father mentioned our legacy or how proud he was of me. He was proud because I was living out the life he wanted for himself. I was ready to tell him that I was done being the castle chef, that I wanted to work at the bakery and run it and continue our family legacy there, but now wasn't the time nor the place.

Elowyn laughed at something her nan said, and my gaze was once again drawn to her infectious light. Right now, more than anything, I just wanted to sweep her up in my arms and dance. And why shouldn't I? It was a dance, and if my father asked about it, I could tell him it was to show that the Wolverns and Carraghs could be mature about our rivalry, that we could put aside our differences for the sake of the town.

I stood before I knew what I was doing.

"Where are you going, son?" my father called.

"To dance," I said over my shoulder, not bothering to look back as my gaze locked onto Elowyn and suddenly, I was in front of her, holding out my hand.

She looked up, a question in her eyes.

Her entire family abruptly stopped talking, staring up at me.

Elowyn's nan shook her finger at me. "If you're here to gloat, Wolvern, you can just turn right around. We all know you'd never have pulled this off without our Elowyn."

"Nan," Elowyn said, but I held up my hands.

"She's right. I couldn't have done this without you."

Elowyn's gaze softened.

"I wanted to say thank you . . . and I was hoping to have a dance?"

Elowyne's mother gasped, while her father's upper lip trembled, his thin mustache twitching.

"Of course she's not going to—" Her nan started, but Elowyn hopped up, grabbing my hand.

"Yes," she said, breathless as I led her to the dance floor while her family sputtered behind us.

I caught my sister's gaze, and she gave me a nod of approval, the smile on her face bigger than I'd seen in a long time. I'd told her my plan to quit the royal chef job, and she'd never been happier.

With Elowyn's hand in mine, I led her to the dance floor, right as the musicians began to play a slow, melodic song, everyone now swaying with their partners.

I placed my hand in the small of her back while holding the other one out in the air.

"I can't believe you asked me to dance," she said. "You are full of surprises."

"I learned from the best," I said.

"Quick. Look over my shoulder and tell me what my family is doing."

I cleared my throat and peeked over her head, all of them staring at us, mouths agape.

"I think we might've actually shocked them into silence? Broken their brains?" I whirled her around as she laughed. "Your turn. What is my father doing?"

She arched her neck to look over my shoulder. "About the same."

"We pulled it off, Carragh. We actually did it."

"With a little help from the sentient kitchen."

Her words brought up images of my face between her legs while the kitchen worked all around us. I had to admit, I could get used to this. To actually enjoying my life after so long of living just for this job.

"Do you want to take a walk tomorrow?" I asked.

Elowyn arched a brow as I spun her. "A walk?"

"Yeah," I said. "A walk."

"Nothing else?" she asked, and I laughed.

"Nothing else."

"But why?"

I laughed again. "Because, believe it or not, I like you. And I'd like to spend time with you. I'd like to walk with you through the snowy streets of Fairwitch and talk and hear more about how your fascinating brain works."

Her cheeks turned pink, and I loved that I could make her blush, not something she did often.

"Okay," she said in a soft voice. "Let's take a walk."

"You ninny!" Elowyn's Nan's voice cut through the room, everyone stopping to stare at the commotion.

"Oh, here we go again," Prince Cillian muttered from where he sat on his throne.

"Oh no." Elowyn's fingers dug into my shoulder.

My father and her nan stood nose-to-nose between the long tables that filled the hall.

"Don't you call me a ninny," my father roared. "Your granddaughter fed some potion to my son. I know it. He's been acting strange ever since she stepped foot in his kitchen."

Elowyn's nan jabbed him in the chest, and he took a few steps backward. "She doesn't need a potion to enchant him. He's probably so used to spending time with you that my granddaughter was a fresh breath of air."

Well, she wasn't wrong about that.

Elowyn sent me a worried look. "What do we do?" she whispered. "Should we intervene?"

"This is their problem." I tightened my hold on her. "They're adults and can figure it out themselves."

Elowyn's mother sobbed into her father's shoulder. "I can't believe she's dancing with that Wolvern boy." Her mother let out a wail while he patted her and glared daggers at Elowyn.

Everyone was still staring, watching the debacle unfold, Prince Cillian sprawled lazily over this throne. I suspected the only reason he didn't stop this was because it was entertaining. His brother, Wolfe, stood next to him, hand hovering over his sword like one of them might attack the high prince.

Wolfe was always prepared, his obsession with protecting his brother overshadowing every other part of his life.

"You're just jealous as always that my boy got the job and your granddaughter didn't."

Elowyn groaned.

"You're just jealous that your son is so bad at his job that Elowyn had to help with the feast."

A few people sucked in sharp breaths at the jab.

"This is getting out of hand," Elowyn said.

A vein popped in my father's neck. "How dare you! And how dare your granddaughter come in and change traditional dishes." He picked up a bowl of cranberry sauce, which Elowyn had added maple and bourbon to. It was fucking delicious.

From here, I could see the way his words affected her nan, who swallowed thickly. "She did what? That cranberry sauce is a family recipe, one served every year at Winter Solstice." She tried to take the bowl from my father, who yanked it back toward his body.

"Stop it," he said.

"Let me have the bowl," she yelled.

"No," he yelled back.

"Okay." Prince Cillian finally stood, wobbling a bit with a goblet of wine sloshing in his grip. "Maybe just put the cranberry sauce—"

Before he could finish, Elowyn's nan yanked it so hard that my father lurched forward with the bowl, shoving it right into Ms. Carragh's cream-colored dress. Gasps arose throughout the room as Elowyn's nan tipped backward, my father going down with her.

Both of them crashed into the table, all the dishes flying in every direction and clattering to the floor, splattering against townspeople who shrieked and dove to avoid the carnage.

"Get off me, you ingrate!" Elowyn's nan yelled while Elowyn's father scrambled to help her.

"I'm trying!" my father yelled back, but every time he attempted to push himself off her, his hands slipped on the wine that had spilled all over the table.

"Well, there goes Winter Solstice," someone muttered.

"Why do the Carraghs and Wolverns always have to ruin things?" a little girl asked her mother, who shushed her while glaring at my father and Elowyn's nan.

The prince's mouth fell open, while Wolfe stepped forward, his face red, his fists clenched. "Enough!" he roared.

Everyone froze, silence descending upon the room. Elowyn and I rushed forward, both of us grabbing the arms of our respective family members, and yanking them away from each other.

"He started it!" Nan yelled. "He's always goading me."

"Oh, please," my father said.

"Will you just shut up?" I snapped, my last thread of calm breaking. "Both of you." I cut a glare at Elowyn's nan, Elowyn staring at me with wide eyes. "I'm so sick of this fighting. Elowyn and I just worked our asses off for the last week preparing this meal, and you two just had to ruin it. You couldn't help yourselves. And you didn't just ruin it for us." I gestured to the mess of food and drink around us. "You ruined it for everyone. Winter Solstice is supposed to be a time when we gather to thank the godwitches for everything they've given us. For this wonderful magic that's infused into our world. This magic that makes our castle sentient, that gives us the ability to hide from the rest of the world so no one discovers our magic and tries to take it."

My father still hadn't spoken. No one had, everyone now listening to me, the room so silent my voice echoed.

"It's not just about that, though." I raked a hand through my hair, thinking of Elowyn and how much joy she'd brought into my life over the last week. "The godwitches preached that we must lean on each other, that we must celebrate each other's gifts and strengths and that we must forgive each other's weaknesses. Each godwitch had their own special magic, but they still relied on each other, used all their magic together to create amazing things. We're supposed to do that too. We're supposed to use this night to reflect on what we're thankful for and how we can all use our abilities to strengthen our community."

The same way Elowyn and I had each used our strengths to make this amazing feast happen.

My father raised his chin, stubbornness laced through his features. "And what are you thankful for?"

I was about to say Elowyn's name when she jumped forward. "He's thankful we didn't kill each other this last week."

Laughter rippled throughout the room, the tension easing some.

"And Liam is right. You two should be ashamed," Elowyn said. "We managed to put aside our differences and deliver this feast, and you couldn't do the same tonight? You couldn't let us have this one night of peace?"

My father's shoulders slumped ever so slightly, and Elowyn's nan looked down at her feet, so uncharacteristic of the old woman.

That had been the end of the fight.

The rest of the night was spent cleaning the mess made, eventually everyone shuffling out of the great hall, spirits mostly recovered after that whole debacle. I grabbed Elowyn's arm before she could leave and pulled her behind a column, dousing us in shadows.

"Are you okay?" I asked.

Her eyes welled with tears. "How are we ever going to make this work?"

I swallowed thickly because I'd been thinking the same thing. Maybe we would have the courage to chase our dreams, but it was too much to hope we could have each other as well, not when our families just could not help themselves. A simple dance had triggered that awful brawl.

"You know what I'm most thankful for?" she said in a small voice.

I pressed my forehead to hers, and she sucked in a shuddering breath. "I'm pretty sure I do," I said. "Because what I'm most thankful for? Getting snowed in with you."

"You stole my answer," she whispered.

"Elowyn?" her mother called from somewhere in the great hall.

These shadows couldn't hide us forever.

"I have to go." She shot me an apologetic look.

"Are we still on for our walk tomorrow?"

She bit her lip. "I don't know, Liam. We might need to just slow things down, think through the repercussions of our actions."

I nodded, trying to blink back the tears that sprang to my eyes.

She gave me one last kiss, a kiss that felt suspiciously like a goodbye, then walked away, disappearing back into the great hall while I pressed my back against the column.

I didn't want to slow things down. I didn't want to hide my feelings for her. I thought about our time together in the kitchen, how seamlessly everything had gone when we worked together. How the kitchen had come alive with magic like I'd never seen before. What we had was special, and when we cooked together, amazing things happened.

I jolted with the realization, a plan forming, a risky one, but if it worked, it would be worth it.

It was time for a visit with the high prince.

Twenty

ELOWYN

I scrubbed a stubborn stain on the wooden bar top inside the Deerborn. The Winter Solstice disaster had happened a week ago, and our business was suffering more than usual, probably because everyone was still mad at Nan for her part in ruining the celebration. The bakery next door hadn't done much better. I hadn't seen hardly any customers visiting, but it gave me no pleasure.

I also hadn't seen much of Liam. He was back in the castle kitchen, busy cooking for the high prince, and we'd agreed that we both needed to come clean with our families first about our intentions with our careers before we even thought about broaching the topic of a relationship between us.

But, godwitches, I missed him.

I missed his fresh doughy scent. I missed the way he kept me organized and on task. I missed talking to him. I missed kissing him. I missed how he was just as excited about my ideas as I was.

"Scrub that spot any harder, and you're going to rub a hole right through the counter," Wolfe said from his usual spot at the end of the bar, a steaming cup of tea in front of him.

I straightened and flipped the rag over my shoulder. "Just want to make sure it's clean."

He stared at me, his dark eyes unreadable as he stroked his thick beard. "You know, you've been unusually quiet this last week."

I was surprised Wolfe had noticed. He kept to himself so much that most times I forgot he was even here.

I cleared my throat and trailed a finger over the grooves of the wood. "Can you blame me after what happened at the feast?"

He shook his head. "No, not really. Just wondering why you and Liam haven't been cooking together since it seemed like you made such a great team."

My head snapped up. "What would you know about me and Liam?"

"I spent the entire feast standing by Cillian's side, watching for danger, and do you know what I saw?"

I shook my head, unsure where he was going with this.

"I saw Liam staring at you. At first I was worried maybe he was planning something devious, the way you Wolverns and Carraghs always do. But then, as Cillian chattered on about how well you two had worked together, how maybe this was a new beginning for your families, I realized he was staring at you because he couldn't tear his eyes away."

Tears sprang to my eyes at Wolfe's eloquent words. I'd never heard him say so much in one sitting.

"Really?" I asked, though it wasn't surprising. I'd had a hard time keeping my gaze off him too.

He'd looked so dashing in those striped purple trousers that were fitted perfectly, a silken purple shirt tucked in with black buttons, the first few undone so I could see that glorious chest I loved to splay my palms against.

"Really." Wolfe grunted. "If I looked at a woman like that, I wouldn't be avoiding her."

I groaned and looked behind me, but no one was in the kitchen. They all must've been upstairs in our family apartment.

"Our families hate each other."

"Who gives a fuck?" Wolfe asked. "Life is precious." His voice quivered, and I knew he was thinking about his younger brother who'd died years ago. "You never know when it's going to be your last chance to see someone, to touch them, to tell them you love them."

The word shot straight to my chest like an arrow. I didn't know if I loved Liam yet, but could I? Yes. I knew without a doubt I could fall so deeply for him I'd never recover.

"Don't waste the time you have being unhappy. And you have been unhappy," Wolfe said.

"Is it that obvious?"

He arched a thick brow. "Your idea of a good time is sneaking spices into your family's mashed potatoes recipe. Does that seem like the actions of a happy person?"

I laughed at the observation, but internally, my mind was reeling. What would happen if I died tomorrow? What would I have to show for it? I hadn't spent a single moment of my thirty years doing anything for myself. I'd lived to please my family, to keep the peace, to keep things fun and light, all to avoid hurting anyone's feelings or causing problems. But the problems existed anyway, and they'd keeping existing, no matter what.

"Just tell them how you feel," Wolfe said. "I wish I'd told Lor how much he meant to me. Before he died."

"Why do you care so much?" I asked. It wasn't like we were friends. He was just a regular who rarely spoke.

He snorted. "For one, I'm sick of your families always fighting, and I'm hoping if you and Liam come together, it'll pave the way for a new future between the Carraghs and Wolverns. Second, my brother is roping me into some idiotic mission."

My ears perked up. No one left Fairwitch. It was too dangerous—if an outsider saw someone emerging from some invisible barrier, it would cause questions, concerns. People left only when they had special permission, and many measures were taken to keep it safe. If the high prince was leaving, this must be very important.

"Mission?" I asked.

Wolfe rolled his eyes. "He thinks his future queen is trapped in some tower, and we have to go rescue her. Some damsel in distress."

I smiled, thinking about grumpy Wolfe trailing his sunshine brother as they went on a rescue mission together. What I wouldn't give to be a fly on the wall for that journey.

"So what does that have to do with me and Liam?"

"While Cillian and I are gone, I need your families to behave. Can't have the lot of you getting into fights and disrupting the peace without us here to rein you in."

That was a good point.

Wolfe slammed a few coins on the table and stood, his massive frame taking up so much space. "Anyway, I just want to get this over with. Find this damn woman and bring her back to Fairwitch so Cillian can marry her and stop harping about it."

I wondered if Wolfe would ever get married, but I doubted it. He was so grumpy, and I wasn't sure there was a woman out there who'd be able to break through the impenetrable walls he put up.

"Just do me a favor and figure it out so I can have one less thing to worry about when we leave." He turned and walked out the door, a blast of wintry wind blowing in, goosebumps raising on my skin.

I chewed the inside of my cheek, thinking through our conversation. Wolfe was right. This was ridiculous, and I was done with it. Done being unhappy and chained.

It didn't even matter what Liam planned to do—I knew what I needed to do for myself.

Nan, Mama, and Papa emerged from the stairs that led up to our apartment. Nan's face fell at the empty restaurant.

I blew out a shaky breath. This wasn't going to be easy, but I had to do it. I opened my mouth to tell them that I was quitting when the door burst open again.

I expected Wolfe to be standing there, saying he forgot something, but Liam stood in the doorway. Sunlight swallowed him, washing him in its golden glow, his blonde hair tousled and falling over his forehead. My heart lurched at the sight of him.

He stepped inside, and his father followed. I stiffened.

"Get your knives," Nan whispered, and my parents made to move.

"No," I said, voice sharp enough that they both stilled.

Liam walked into the tavern, his father trailing him, head hanging. I sent him a questioning look, unsure what was happening.

"I'm sorry I didn't come sooner," he said. "It took a week to get everything finalized, and I was afraid if I saw you, I'd tell you about my plan and get your hopes up before it was approved."

None of what he'd just said made sense.

"What is he talking about, Elowyn?" Mama asked, arms crossed.

Liam shot me a dazzling smile, full of pride. "Your daughter is going to be the new royal chef at the castle."

My heart swelled so big my chest ached from it. "What? How?"

He took another step toward me. "And I'm going to be your sous chef."

His father made a grunt of disapproval behind him, but Liam ignored it, his gaze focused on me.

"But you two can't work together. Wolverns and Carraghs don't mix," Nan protested.

Liam swallowed, not blurting out the words I wanted to. *We do mix. We're a perfect fit.*

"You did all that for me?" I asked, heart stuttering.

He shrugged. "Well, I did it a little for myself too."

"No." Nan shook her head. "We'll talk to the prince and get this sorted out. We'll let him know it's not going to work—"

Her voice cut off abruptly as I flung myself into Liam's arms and pressed a kiss to his lips. Mama fainted somewhere behind us while Nan gasped.

"What is going on?" Eamon said, horror filling his voice.

I didn't care about any of it. I kissed Liam like this might very well be our last day together. I'd kiss him like this every day for the rest of our lives if I could.

I broke off the kiss, turning to see my father fanning Mama's face while Nan glared at me. "So that's what you two have been up to? I knew something was going on, but I didn't want to believe it."

I grabbed Liam's hand. "Yes, and we're proof that the Carraghs and Wolverns can get along. Aren't you all sick of the fighting, the rivalry, the anger?"

"Do you all know why the high prince agreed to this?" Liam asked. "Well, first of all, because he said he'd never tasted better food than at this year's Winter Solstice feast. But second of all because he can't handle any more of the fighting. Fairwitch Isle has enough issues without having to deal with us and our constant shenanigans. Once upon a time, these two business were joined, and they thrived."

His father and Nan both swiveled their heads toward the log wall that separated us from the bakery.

"We could thrive again if we work together, and Elowyn and I are proof of that."

I squeezed his hand as Mama's eyes fluttered open.

"But if you don't want that, then I can't be part of your life anymore." He turned to his father, and I sucked in a sharp breath. "I'll be cordial, no ill will, but I will not let you treat the woman I love badly."

Everything in me went still at that, the world fading to just those words. *The woman I love.*

"Love?" Nan asked.

Mama fainted again, Papa catching her.

We'd known each other a lifetime, but it was only the last few weeks I felt like I'd really gotten to know him, and yet, that word didn't terrify me. It felt . . . right.

"I love you too," I said with a shaky voice.

He kissed me, his hold on me tight, and I knew that my biggest adventure yet was just beginning.

Twenty-One

ELOWYN, TEN MONTHS LATER

Fall bloomed all around us, the rolling green hills surrounding Fairwitch a stark green, the gardens outside the kitchen still in bloom with purple hydrangeas, lemon and lime trees, pink and red rose bushes, and beautifully trimmed hedges. Orange, red, and yellow leaves covered the tall trees, some of them floating to the gardens below.

Liam's strong arms circled around me as I washed a pan in the basin on the counter, gazing out the window that I'd fallen through just ten months earlier.

I inhaled his freshly baked bread scent that I'd never get tired of.

I'd spent the last ten months cooking with him in this kitchen, learning to control my worse impulses while setting free my better ones.

I loved that Liam helped me stay on task and organized while also encouraging my creativity and sense for adventure in the kitchen. I loved working with him.

I loved him. More than I'd ever imagined I could love another person.

I leaned my back into his chest, savoring the feel of his arms around my waist, savoring this simple silence between us.

"Stop looking at me," Barty yelled.

I stiffened.

"The peace and quiet could only last so long," Liam murmured. "They're at it again."

"I would, but you're breathing so loudly I can't help but stare" came Tal's reply.

Across the gardens, our newest resident, Niamh, stalked away from Wolfe, who stared after her with a menacing gaze.

Wolfe and Cillian had found the woman in the tower, after all, and she was possibly the sweetest person I'd ever met, which made it so odd seeing the way Wolfe stared after her right now.

She was sunshine, and he was . . . well, not, but he looked at her like . . . I couldn't quite put my finger on it.

"Someone's got it bad," Liam said, nodding toward Wolfe, fists clenched at his sides.

"What?" I gaped at the guard, still staring after Niamh, chest heaving. "But she's betrothed to his brother."

Cillian had declared he'd found his future bride . . . although there were some obstacles in her way, mainly the castle and all its tricks.

"All I know is what I'm seeing," Liam said. "That's a man in love."

"Wolfe?" I shrieked. "You do know Wolfe, right? The man who won't talk to anyone, who's completely isolated himself, the grumpiest person I know."

"You don't recognize how he's looking after her?"

I squinted, realizing I did recognize it. That was why it had looked so familiar. "He looks at her like you look at me." I turned and looped my arms around Liam's neck, so much love and longing sparking in his brown eyes. "That's going to cause problems between him and his brother."

"Maybe," Liam said. "Or maybe they'll figure it out. Like we worked through our problems."

"For godwitch's sake, stop glaring at me," Barty barked. "I'm just breathing."

I shook my head, trying to ignore the bickering.

"We did do a pretty good job, huh? Squashed a centuries' old rivalry between our families with food."

"And love." Liam leaned down and kissed me, breaking away too soon for my liking. "Although, I don't know if we completely squashed it," he said.

"What do you mean?"

"Last night at dinner, I overheard your nan threatening to stab my father with her fork if he looked at her wrong."

I laughed. "Okay, maybe we haven't completely squashed it."

"Maybe we never will." Liam paused. "Would that bother you?"

"No," I said.

And I meant it. Liam had given me everything I'd wanted but hadn't known that I needed. I'd been withering away until I fell through his kitchen window, and he made me realize how much I deserved to cook the way I wanted, to create what I wanted, and most importantly, how much I needed that for myself.

"At least your nan loves me," Liam said, and I rolled my eyes at the reminder.

It was true. Once Nan had seen how organized Liam was and how he kept me from chasing wild ideas all the time, she'd really warmed up to him. It also didn't hurt that he'd given up the chef job so I could have it.

All of it had won over Nan, and now I was suspicious she actually preferred Liam to me, which was just fine. After a lifetime under her scrutiny, it was nice for her to fuss over someone else for once.

I finished washing the pot, handing it over to Liam, who toweled it dry before setting it on the counter.

Sometimes, the kitchen was nice and washed our dishes for us. Other times, it decided we could do our own.

Apparently today was one of those days. I wondered if it was the sprouts I'd made. They tasted delicious but smelled atrocious, and Castle did not tend to like strong smells. At least it hadn't started a fire like it did with those sardines Perla Wolvern made hundreds of years ago. I'd heard that story from Liam's father at least ten times now.

"Stop blowing leaves at me," Tal yelled at Barty.

"Oh, I'm sorry. I can't hear you over my loud breathing," Barty said back.

I just shook my head and turned to see a stack of cups, all of them upside down, sitting on the island.

I scowled, looking up. "Really, Castle?" We were on a first-name basis now, and as long as I didn't cook sardines, I felt comfortable addressing Castle without the worry it would excommunicate me. "I just put all the dishes away. Why are these cups out?"

Liam stood by the table, and I could've sworn a nervous look passed across his face.

Maybe he was having an anxiety flare. They happened less frequently since I took over as chef, but if they did occur, instead of needing to run in the blistering cold to shed his anxious thoughts, he'd been practicing healthier coping techniques like breathing and grounding himself. His hands pressed into the wooden counter, and I gave him a nod of assurance and a smile as I grabbed each tin cup, flipping them over one by one so they could be put away.

Flip. Flip. Flip. Fli—I froze when I flipped the last cup. I didn't fully get it turned over, so it clattered to its side, rolling away while I stared at the glittering brass key on the table that had been hiding underneath.

I picked it up, the metal cold against my fingers. "What is this?"

I turned to Liam, nerves now gone from his face as he smiled broadly. "It's yours if you want it."

I looked down at the key, then up again at him, then down at the key, and he laughed.

He strode toward me and turned me toward him. He tipped my chin up with his thumb. "I want you to move into my cottage, to marry me, to love me . . . forever."

Tears sprang to my eyes. "You and Castle worked together on this?"

"It was my idea!" Tal shouted.

"No, it absolutely was not," Barty said.

"I distinctly remember saying it first."

"Yes," Liam said over their bickering, "along with the gargoyles, whose opinions I didn't really ask but that they gave anyway."

"Did not!" Barty shouted.

"Will our families panic?" I asked.

"Oh, absolutely," Liam said with a smirk. "But I'd like to think of that as a perk. It'll be fun after all the torment they've put us through."

I stared at the key, turning it over in my palm.

Liam had the cottage built when he'd first gotten the chef job and could finally move out of the apartment over his family bakery. It stood among the rolling hills behind the castle, a beautiful view of the entire city of Fairwitch and the green swaths of land that went as far as the eye could see.

I thought about all the twists and turns it had taken to get us to this point.

"This was definitely not love at first sight," I murmured. "But we got there eventually."

"You still haven't said yes," Liam said.

"You don't already know?" I asked, gaze snapping to meet his. "Yes." I kissed his jaw. "Yes." I kissed his nose. "Yes." I kissed his cheek. "Yes," I whispered as my lips touched his in a blissful happiness I would never tire of.

 **Next in Series: This Damsel Is Not in Distress**—a cozy, spicy romantasy about a woman chosen by a sentient castle to be its queen and her growing feelings for the body-guard that might just ruin it all. **Pre-order now to get 50% off and a free gift** at https://teeharlowe.com/products/damsel-ebook or use the QR code above!

Keep reading for a sneak peek!

This Damsel Is Not in Distress Sneak Peek

NIAMH

Something was wrong, and my belly swooped at the ominous feeling niggling at me.

I sat in my stuffed armchair, blanket across my lap, a book in hand, looking around the tower that had become my home over the last three years. Books filled the shelves curving across the walls, organized by color and size. Sun shone through the tall windows lining the stairs that spiraled up to the second floor.

I wrinkled my nose, inhaling the earthy, mossy scents that filled the little room. I shifted in my chair, the skirt of my dark blue dress bunching under my legs. Nothing was amiss outwardly, but I could've sworn I felt the slightest tremble beneath me. I could go to the windows to see whether there was anything to be concerned about, but then I might actually witness a threat, and what would I do then? I wouldn't be able to fight it—I didn't have a sword, and even if I did, I'd be more likely to stab myself with it than someone else.

Panic jolted through me as a terrifying thought hit: It could be the Brotherhood of Magic, come to take my tower from me, the fearsome Butcher of the Brotherhood leading the charge. I didn't hear any yelling outside, and there was no evidence of people lurking about.

I chewed at my lip, glancing around the tower and studying each part, from the bookshelves to the rug to the stairs winding around the wall. A few books fell to the floor, then fluttered upward, inserting themselves back onto the shelves. This was a magical tower, so maybe it was using some magic I couldn't see.

It did that sometimes.

Moved itself away from the sun or toward it, depending on its mood. Sometimes it opened its roof to give me a perfect view of the starry sky. The tower could do anything it wanted—anything I wanted—which was why it made the perfect home, the perfect place to keep me safe.

My stomach rumbled, and I realized I'd been so caught up in my thoughts that I'd forgotten about dinner. I snapped my fingers, chuckling quietly. That must've been what was wrong. The tower wasn't in any kind of danger. I was just hungry and not thinking clearly.

I'd have to remedy that. "Tower," I called. "I'm ready for dinner."

Before my eyes, the cylinder stone tower transformed into a round dining hall with a long cherry-wood table. Beneath me, my armchair became a dining chair. Food appeared from thin air in front of me: roasted leg of lamb with sautéed squash and whipped ricotta cream.

"You could warn me before you do that, you know," a voice said from the book still sitting on my lap.

I glanced down at Morton, his sleek, pink, scaled body tucked into the crevice between the pages, his eyes blinking sleepily as he gazed at me.

I grabbed the book and set it on the table next to my plate, then shook out a napkin and laid it across my lap. "I thought you were sleeping."

The bookwyrm's shaggy pink eyebrows bunched. "I *was* sleeping. Then someone's stomach rumbled as loud as a clap of thunder and awoke me."

"Ah, so it wasn't the tower transforming that awoke you but my stomach." I lifted the leg of lamb and took a bite, speaking through a mouthful of delectable meat. "I can't really help that, now can I?"

He harrumphed and slithered from the book to the table, forked tongue poking out toward my plate.

I swatted at him. "You get your own food." I glanced at the full plate doubtfully. "On second thought, this is a lot. We're going to have to take a walk after this."

His tail rose in the air, shaking back and forth behind him. "As long as it's not on a cliffside again. It was so windy last time, I almost fell over the edge and straight into the sea."

I cocked my head. "You do know you can't die in this tower, right?"

For the smallest second, my chest grew tight. At least I didn't think it was possible. Thoughts of those earlier trembles entered my mind, that tight feeling growing more taut, making my muscles feeling like they might snap. I'd seen this tower transform into hundreds of places and environments, and never once had I been in enough danger to question my mortality.

I was fine. This was fine. Everything. Was. Fine.

His pink eyebrows shot up. "And how would you know? Have you ever tried to die in here?"

I stuffed another big bite into my mouth, unable to stop myself as I said the next command: "Tower, I'm done with dinner."

Morton let out a yelp as he fell from the disappearing table to the dark purple rug, and I scurried to the bookshelves unraveling on the wall. They were filled with books and journals, each one making a little *pop* sound as it appeared from thin air. I grabbed a green cloth journal and pulled it out, flipping it open to a blank page before I lost my train of thought. As I pondered we could die, the exact question in my brain appeared on the blank page in dark ink.

Can we die in this tower?

Once I figured out the answer, I'd open the journal and record it here with my thoughts.

"What are you journalling about now?" Morton stretched out his neck and looked at the page where my question had appeared. "Do you need your cloak?" His eyes dipped to the tips of my fingers, which were a bluish-purple. "Maybe you need to sit back in your chair and get a blanket. Or I could get the jar of firebugs—"

"I'm asking if we can die in here," I said, unable to hide the quiver in my voice. My fingers were the least of my concerns right now. They did this sometimes when I got really stressed. "This tower has protected us since we arrived, so it never occurred to me that harm could come to us while inside it."

But I couldn't answer this particular question without actually trying to die—something I very much didn't want to do. The tightness squeezed my lungs, making it hard to breathe.

"You're demented," Morton mumbled. "Being stuck in this tower for three years has addled your brain."

"We're not stuck in here." My gaze flicked to a statue of Samara that sat on the mantel over the fireplace. The hearth godwitch stared back with her blank eyes, a broom in her hand and her red hair tied back under a scarf. The hearth godwitch was the plainest of all the godwitches, but her magic was not. I looked around at the tower fueled by her magic. "He didn't mean it," I said to the statue. "We don't feel stuck. We're very grateful to be here under your protection."

Morton blinked. "You know the godwitches have been gone for thousands of years, right? It's just a statue. Samara can't actually hear you."

"She might be gone, but her magic is not." I pointed at the tower as proof. "So let's keep our unkind comments to ourselves," I said with an edge to my voice, unable to handle the thought of getting kicked out of our home because we'd insulted it.

"Anyway," Morton said, his tail shaking in the air. "My point was that you're too focused on this. Who wants to think about the possibility of dying?"

I snapped the journal full of questions closed. I didn't want to think about dying—the very thought of it was what had driven me to find this tower and lock myself inside. It was what had driven me to stay here for three long years without attempting to venture out. "It's just a scientific query," I told the bookwyrm, then pointed to the books on the shelves, all of which had been here when we'd arrived.

"I'm excited to keep learning about this tower and its abilities. That's all."

No need to mention the tremble to Morton. He'd probably tell me I was imagining things, and to be fair, I probably was.

This tower was one of the most wondrous feats of magic I'd ever seen, magic that Samara and all the godwitches had given up and forced into our world, into objects and creatures and nature, before they disappeared.

I turned from the shelves, coming face-to-face with the empty grey hearth, which conjured a memory of a very different hearth. One full of terrifying magical flames. Tall and hungry ones that I'd run from as they burned everything I loved to the ground. My heart stuttered, my fingers turning a deeper purple. I ground my teeth and whirled around, trying to push those awful memories away.

That was the downside to this world of magic—it made people greedy, hungry for the most powerful objects or creatures. It made people willing to do terrible things to possess that power.

I sniffled and strode back toward the chair, looking away from the hearth, determined to shed myself of whatever anxiety was riddling me. *Deep breaths.* That's what my mother had always said when these panic attacks came on. Sometimes it worked. Sometimes it didn't and things escalated to the point where I thought I might actually die from the anxiety. Thankfully, this time my slow breathing was working, and the tightness loosened, my breaths coming easier.

Morton slithered into my lap and looked up at me with his wide black eyes, the only part of his body that wasn't pink. The hard edges of his dragon-like face softened. "We're not going to die, Niamh. We've survived this long, and we'll keep surviving."

I tipped my head toward a light blue book on the floor. "Tell me again what that one said about the tower's magic." *Let it go, Niamh. Just let it go.* I didn't need to ruminate on this, to trigger another panic attack, but my brain and mouth were not on the same page. "Maybe it mentions death somewhere in there?"

If a bookwyrm could roll his eyes, that was what I imagined Morton would be doing right now. Instead, he let out a heavy sigh and slithered down the chair and toward the blue book, flipping it open with his tail.

The book splayed open, pages fluttering as Morton hinged opened his cavernous jaw and began to eat each page that flipped past him. I'd known the little bookwyrm for two decades, and it never got old watching his magic at work. He inhaled the pages until every single one was gone, his stomach bulging, his body stiff.

This was it, his magic at work.

He heaved, all the pages regurgitating out of his mouth in pieces that looked like a puzzle. The pieces put themselves back together into pages that wove into the hardcover binding until the book was exactly as it had been, no evidence of being eaten remaining.

Morton turned his head with a huff. "The tower can grant those in its residence anything they want as long as they never leave its walls. Shall the resident vacate the premises, all the magic of the tower will no longer be at their disposal and they will not be granted reentry."

I wrinkled my nose. "It didn't mention anything about death?"

He sighed. "Do you think I'd miss something like that? I ate every page! Everything else was all about the magic the tower can and cannot do: cannot summon people, cannot create something that doesn't already exist, cannot possess a person or creature, cannot be destroyed by traditional means, i.e., cannonball, fire, flood, etc. Although, interestingly enough, it did mention something about challenging someone to a fight, and in that event—"

"Okay, that's enough." I rubbed my temples, a headache forming.

Morton glided to my foot and back up into my lap. "I do think we'll eventually have to leave the tower, you know."

I jolted, my stomach flipping at the suggestion. "Why would you say that?"

The bookwyrm arched one of his shaggy brows. "You think we're going to stay here forever?"

"Well, why not?" I petted the armchair like it was an old friend. "This tower can give us anything."

And we were protected from all the dangers of the outside world, dangers we couldn't protect ourselves from.

Morton's tail undulated behind him. "Except other people, friendships, love, a life."

I'd had all those once, and I'd lost them. No, that wasn't quite right. I hadn't fought for them. Hadn't been brave enough to do so. I was better off here, where I didn't have to become anyone's burden.

"You're a wyrm," I said, "why do you need any of those things?"

"I don't." He stared at me pointedly with large glassy black eyes that had far too much depth and knowledge buried in them.

"We do have lives." I pointed to the bookshelves. "We live a thousand lives through these books. You're a bookwyrm. You of all creatures should love access to endless stories."

He raised the upper half of his body into the air. "I think at this point you're more of a bookworm than I am." He paused, a heavy pause that indicated he had more to say. "And I think you like this tower a little too much." His black eyes narrowed to slits.

I bristled, his words hitting much too close to the truth. "What does that mean? Who wouldn't like this tower? It's some of the most amazing magic that exists on the entire continent of Aubergn."

"Right, but it doesn't have any other people. You're perfectly content to sit alone in a tower for the rest of your life. That's not normal, Niamh."

I scoffed. It was like he was forgetting why we were in this tower in the first place. But I could never forget. "Maybe for someone who hasn't been through what I have it isn't, but I like it here. We're safe, and I get to read books all day and talk to you."

"More like annoy me," he mumbled, and I shot him a glare. "It's not healthy for you."

I looked down at my curvy body, thick thighs, and pudgy stomach —all more filled out than they had been years ago. "I'm perfectly healthy, thank you very much. I walk three times a day."

All I had to do was think about walking and the tower would transform into a meadow or a forest or, much to Morton's annoyance, a cliffside.

The end of his pink tail flicked my stomach. "I don't mean physically. I mean mentally. You're a human. You're meant to have community. I'm afraid you'll never find a home if you don't overcome your fears."

I shifted the blanket over my lap, not wanting to talk about this anymore. "Want to get me another book?" I asked, voice airy, unconcerned. "The one about the king and the peasant girl who tricks him into giving away his crown?"

Morton sighed and slithered toward the bookshelves and up the wall. "You've read that one at least ten times."

"And I'll read it ten times more." I liked the peasant girl, so clever and brave, so willing to fight for herself and those she loved.

A book plopped in my lap, Morton already opening it for me. "Are you avoiding this conversation?"

I pinched the bridge of my nose. Maybe if I agreed with him, he'd stop with all of this, and I could get lost in a different world. "Fine, we'll leave the tower one day, okay? One day we will venture out and see what has become of Aubergn." I snuggled deeper into the chair, determined to forget about that stupid tremble that I'd definitely imagined. "But that day will absolutely not be today."

Pre-order now!

www.ingramcontent.com/pod-product-compliance
Lightning Source LLC
Chambersburg PA
CBHW021554150726
47990CB00006B/2542